At 36, Ian MacKintosh is well-est
and screen-writer, but is perhaps b
television series and its compleme
Officer, he takes pains to keep his r
up-to-date and additionally revisit
before writing this, his eighth nove
as his primary fascination outside t
London home with an ever-increasi llection of model
airliners. He was awarded the M.B.E. in the Birthday
Honours List, 1976

By the same author

A SLAYING IN SEPTEMBER

COUNT NOT THE COST

A DRUG CALLED POWER

THE MAN FROM DESTINY

THE BRAVE CANNOT YIELD

WARSHIP

HMS HERO

Ian MacKintosh

Warship: Holt, R.N.

Futura Publications Limited
A Contact Book

A Contact Book

First published in 1977
by Futura Publications Limited
in association with Arthur Barker Limited

ISBN 0 8600 7490 0
Printed in Great Britain by
Hazell Watson & Viney Ltd
Aylesbury, Bucks

Futura Publications Limited
110 Warner Road
Camberwell, London SE5

For David McTaggart, whose Pacific voyages inspired the story, and for David Cunliffe, who sails on a pond at Hampstead.

CONTENTS

PART ONE: COLOURS . . .

PART TWO: . . . AND SUNSET

AUTHOR'S NOTE

I wrote this book – as is now my practice – in a relatively short time, sandwiched (pace my publisher) between WARSHIP scripts.

I began it with the same attitude, towards nuclear tests and protesters, that I had held as a Naval Officer: namely that testing is necessary; and that protesters are naive.

In the same short time, however, I have modified my views; and modified them because – in researching the book – I was obliged for the first time to examine the whole issue. And I hope that, in addition to being entertained, the reader may be similarly prompted to look again at the arguments.

Deliberately, I have not named in the story the country responsible for the testing. Those who believe it to be France could not be blamed for so doing; but I trust that – in consequence of the *Vega* protests and other pressures – the French will never again bring atmospheric testing to the Pacific.

I trust. I may be very wrong.

I.M.

Part One

COLOURS . . .

CHAPTER ONE

WELCOME TO HONG KONG

Holt came often to the ship's bridge in harbour.

Attracted by the very fact that it was, on such occasions, still and deserted, he would climb into his high Captain's chair and treasure a moment of solitude and self-communion, while below him, one deck down, a veritable legion of callers would knock on his door, find the cabin empty and retire in disappointment, annoyance or relief.

Now, with HMS *Hero* berthed alongside in the Hong Kong Naval Base, this practice of escape held particular pleasure. In front of him, framed in the wide bridge windows and lit by the promise of a May morning, Victoria Harbour was an ever-changing kaleidoscope of bustle and activity: ships, junks and ferries criss-crossed endlessly and stitched colourful patterns on the water and the imagination; to port, the skyscrapers of Hong Kong Island marched spectacularly all the way upwards to the top of the Peak; to starboard – across the harbour and beyond the matching skyscrapers of Kowloon – purple mountains rose as majestically to peer into the forbidden mainland of China.

And Holt thought of it all in these terms.

Captain Edward Kelvin Holt was forty-three, and a man whose considerable intelligence and deep sensitivity set him apart from the day-to-day boisterousness of service life. Yet there was about him an air of subdued power and calm control, with determination in the jawline, watchfulness in the sad eyes, economy in every movement. He knew himself completely, was fully conversant with his own strengths and weaknesses and abode almost fiercely by his own old-fashioned convictions. The sorrows of the past were kept locked away in the innermost recesses of mind and heart, seldom to be examined, never to be brooded upon, never to be apportioned to others in blame or recrimination.

He maintained a passionate belief in the Navy, took personal and professional satisfaction from his job and was committed to making a success of his time in command of HMS *Hero* – not for his greater glorification, but simply because he was paid to do so.

It had been a very long time since Holt knew real happiness, but he was content on that May morning in Hong Kong, with two thousand six hundred tons of frigate – his frigate – beneath his feet. Yet there was in him that morning, too, a strange anticipation, an indefinable premonition that things were about to happen.

And he was right.

In Holt's night-cabin, Thomas Meryon – a visiting Member of Parliament – was finishing breakfast.

In the Excelsior Hotel, a girl was dressing for work.

In a yacht marina on the south side of the Island, a man was preparing his boat for a voyage.

In the air, a hundred miles from Hong Kong, a Royal Air Force passenger aircraft was on the last leg of its long pilgrimage from England.

Paths were about to intersect. Lives were about to intertwine.

Destinies were being decided.

Across the bay – parked illegally in front of Hong Kong's international airport at Kai Tak – Lieutenant

Paul Peek and Leading Regulator Pat Fuller, in white day uniform, sat in a borrowed naval landrover and watched an aircraft make its final approach.

'This is it,' Peek said confidently.

Fuller looked sideways at the young Lieutenant. They were awaiting the RAF VC-10 and Peek had already announced its arrival three times, misidentifying in turn a Cathay Pacific Tristar, an All-Nippon 727 and a Northwest Orient 747.

'Sir,' volunteered Fuller in his quiet Scots voice, adding a scratch at his red hair for effect, 'I reckon you're a better navigator than a plane-spotter.' And to stress the opinion: 'Otherwise, we'd never have got to Hong Kong.'

'What is it, then?'

'Another seven-two-seven.'

'It isn't,' Peek denied.

It was.

Fuller grinned. 'We'll bet on the next one.'

But the next one *was* the VC-10. And, interest sharpened by the fact that they were concerned with one of its passengers, Peek and Fuller watched closely as it approached the chequerboard – a marker set high on a mountain, on which aircraft turned for Kai Tak's runway one-three. The VC-10 duly made its turn, seemingly – to the watching pair – by clawing itself off the hillside; then scraped the Kowloon roof-tops in descent, hurtled over the boundary-fence and on to the concrete ribbon of runway, jutting out for eleven-thousand feet into Kowloon Bay.

Fuller expelled his breath noisily. 'Glad I came by ship.'

'Too right,' Peek nodded thoughtfully. 'Hope our new Number One brought a change of underpants.'

But in fact their new First Lieutenant, Lieutenant-Commander James Napier, was composed and unperturbed when he stepped off the aircraft. A tall, good-looking man of thirty-four, Napier was a devastating combination of charm, grace, efficiency and unconventionality. A bachelor, and the only son of a wealthy farmer, he regarded the Navy as the best club in the world, and stayed in the service simply because he enjoyed the life.

Yet there was another side to Napier. Playboy he might be; but fop he was not. He was a mine-warfare and clearance-diving officer by specialisation, and wore the George Medal for bravery in bomb-disposal. A brilliant seaman, a clever tactician and a natural leader, his only real weakness – if it *was* a weakness – was that he knew his worth, and suffered fools not at all.

Dressed now in a white polo-neck sweater and blue denim suit, and with his brown hair slightly too long for most Naval tastes, he might not have been instantly recognisable as a Lieutenant-Commander, but the steel and the authority were there, sitting easily beneath the amused smile.

By the time Peek and Fuller had fought the traffic in the streets between the commercial airport and the RAF section of the field, Napier was clearing Customs and walking out into the morning sunshine. Peek, who had served with him before, recognised him and crossed to meet him.

'Welcome to Hong Kong, sir.'

'Hello, Paul.'

And then Fuller had joined them, to take Napier's luggage. Peek introduced the Leading Regulator and was glad to see that Napier shook Fuller's hand readily and genuinely. It was as Peek had remembered: Napier was 'new Navy'; no believer in 'us and them'. And it was as well – Holt had taught *Hero* to function on understated discipline and the basics of compatibility.

Napier looked to Peek. 'What's your function in our mighty steamer?'

'Navigating Officer.'

'Oh.' Napier's eyes went to Fuller. 'How did you ever find Hong Kong?'

'We've done that bit, sir,' laughed Fuller. 'It's now "be kind to Lieutenant Peek" week.'

'That's what you think.' Napier climbed into the landrover. 'His hell is just beginning.'

Fuller laughed again, got in and started up. For a time, he drove sedately – to enable Napier to drink in the colour and atmosphere – but sedateness was not Fuller's style, especially behind a wheel, and before long he was performing his usual illegalities in Ma Tau Wei Road, orchestrating a blare of indignant horns from the rest of the Kowloon morning rush-hour.

He hauled the landrover out and around a large truck overloaded with live chickens, and accelerated away to leave behind a combined protest from startled poultry and squealing brakes. Then grinned. 'Wonder if they can turn purple with rage.'

'Who?' asked Peek.

'Chinese drivers.'

'Don't,' instructed Napier, 'take your eyes off the road to find out.' He half-turned to Peek. 'Anyone else on board I'd know?'

'Bill Kiley, the Weapons Electrics Officer.'

'Ah, yes.' Napier nodded in satisfaction. 'Bill's a good hand.'

'And,' Peek added weightily, 'we have a visiting Member of Parliament.'

Napier's face clouded. 'I heard. Thomas Albert Meryon. Thumper of tubs and purveyor of hot air.'

'Right,' Peek agreed. 'He said he'd met you.'

Napier nodded again. 'At a dinner at Greenwich. We exchanged words.'

'Oh?'

'His were lengthy and on the subject of cutting Defence. Mine were very short and on the subject of cutting throats.'

A chortle escaped Fuller's lips as he stared woodenly ahead. Napier stared at him, then at Peek.

'Don't tell me you've bred a Regulator with a sense of humour?'

Peek shook his head, spoke sadly. 'He got caught in a fire last year, rescuing a Chief Cook. Heat softened his brain.'

'True, sir,' Fuller admitted. 'And now I'm a candidate for officer.'

'True,' Peek confessed, in turn.

Napier laughed. 'I think I may enjoy HMS *Hero*.'

On the flight deck of HMS *Hero*, Holt was watching a red taxi come around the basin to approach the ship. His interest was merely passing – until the taxi drew up at the foot of the gangway, and a young woman alighted. Such a caller was unusual on a weekday forenoon, and Holt remained watching as she came inboard.

He saw that she was in her late twenties or early thirties, with long red hair and an attractive, engagingly-freckled face. Her slim figure was revealed to good advantage by her blue shirt and scarlet slacks, and she carried a voluminous and purposeful handbag.

Whether or not he experienced anything else in that first moment, he was never able to say. Certainly, there was no clash of cymbals, no fanfare of trumpets.

But there was surprise. For instead of approaching the quartermaster, as he had expected her to do, she strode boldly across the flight deck, faced him squarely and asked: 'Are you the Captain of HMS *Hero*?'

Holt nodded. 'Edward Holt.'

'Zoe Carter.' She thrust a hand at him, in a peculiarly mannish gesture that was not at all in keeping with the femininity of her voice and bearing. 'I'm a freelance reporter, to agencies in the UK and US.'

Holt took the hand. 'How do you do?'

'I'd like to see your resident VIP.'

'Mr Meryon?' Holt frowned. 'He *is* on board. But whether he'll see you . . .'

Zoe grinned. 'He'll see me. As the Navy should know, Thomas Meryon never passes up an opportunity to put his name in print.'

Holt was forced into a half-smile. But his tone was expressionless.

'To use the time-honoured expression, Miss Carter – no comment.' He indicated towards the waist of the ship. 'This way.'

He led the girl for'ard, through the screen door and into the cabin flat, where he knocked on the door of the night-cabin, then went in.

Thomas Meryon was in an armchair, his papers spread across what was normally Holt's bunk (in Holt's sleeping quarters); but, of course, the most comfortable accommodation in the ship went to the guest – while Holt contented himself with a camp-bed in the day-cabin, rather than disturb his officers. This, Holt did not resent; but Meryon – in many ways – he did.

Thomas Albert Meryon was forty-eight years old, a polished if somewhat humourless politician, grey-haired, immaculate, and a perennial thorn in the sides of the Armed Forces, and of the Navy in particular.

At first glance, in his smart three-piece grey suit, and with his quiet well-spoken manner, Meryon would have passed as a city barrister or merchant banker, but he was in fact the most vitriolic and tenacious of back-benchers. He had made his name in an unrelenting and often ill-founded crusade against Defence expenditure, and admirals and generals were known to blanch at the depth, detail and persistence of his Parliamentary questions.

But as yet, the Service Chiefs had not given up attempts to woo and pacify Meryon; and when *Hero*, on group-deployment to the Far East with a small force of ships, had been detached from the group and sent into Hong Kong, the Sea Lords had elected – in their wisdom, or lack thereof – to invite Meryon to sojourn in the Orient, and to join *Hero*.

Holt could have taken it as a compliment that he was entrusted with the task of fielding the unpredictable MP, but it was an unwelcome chore and potentially, at least, an explosive one.

Now, Holt smiled to Meryon: 'There's a lady outside, a reporter. If you'd rather not see her, I can divert her elsewhere.'

'Certainly not.' Meryon came to his feet, smiled back. 'The Press can't pick and choose their times, can they?'

He emerged into the flat ahead of Holt, and introduced himself to Zoe with another smile and a firm handshake. And Holt had to admit that Meryon was good: within a few seconds, the man was in control, but in such a way that one would have believed that it was he, Meryon, who was grateful for the interview.

And perhaps, Holt thought sourly, he was. Meryon's

reputation as a headline-seeker was – as Zoe Carter had suggested – well known to all.

Holt offered the roomy day-cabin for the interview, and both Zoe and Meryon pressed him to join them. Thus, all three arranged themselves in armchairs around a coffee-table, on which Zoe placed a portable tape-recorder with an exterior microphone. Holt offered coffee, too, but this was declined almost impatiently by the others as the interview got underway.

Zoe asked Meryon: 'What exactly are you doing in Hong Kong?'

'I want to see for myself,' Meryon responded, 'if there is any real justification for the Navy's presence East of Suez.'

'And you're living in HMS *Hero*?'

'The better to observe.'

Zoe looked to Holt. 'Captain Holt?'

Holt said carefully: 'Mr Meryon is a guest in the ship.'

'But an enemy in the camp?'

'By no means.' Holt tried a grin. 'Mr Meryon is entitled to his opinions. We hope to change them.'

There was a knock and Napier, direct from Kai Tak and still dressed in the denim-suit, pushed aside the door-curtain and looked in. Realising at once that there was some form of meeting in progress, he apologised: 'Oh, excuse me . . .'

But Holt stood up. 'James Napier?'

'Yes, sir.'

'Come in,' Holt said, and crossed to shake Napier's hand. Then, looking at Zoe: 'Lieutenant-Commander James Napier, my new First Lieutenant and second-in-command. Miss Zoe Carter, who is a journalist.'

Napier and Zoe exchanged smiles.

'And,' Holt turned to Meryon, 'Mr Meryon, our visiting Member of Parliament.'

Meryon came reluctantly to his feet, shook hands with Napier, observed: 'We've met, of course.'

'How kind of you, sir,' Napier replied evenly, 'to remember.'

'I remember very well.'

Zoe, sensing the atmosphere between the two men, was at once interested. And as Napier started to excuse himself again, she broke in quickly: 'Would you mind staying?' And to Holt: 'If you've no objection.'

'None,' smiled Holt. He gestured to a chair. 'Sit down, James.'

It was an invitation which Holt was soon to regret, and it was his second mistake, for he had decided already that Zoe Carter would be no match for Meryon.

But then, Holt did not know that Zoe Carter was lining up Meryon for a fall, nor that, although it would take time to achieve and this was but the first step, the crash of it would ultimately reverberate around the world.

CHAPTER TWO

A PRIVATE OPINION

'Not at all.' Meryon responded, in answer to another query from Zoe, 'but war isn't discouraged by ships. It's obviated by good sense and good manners.'

Zoe had her opening. 'Then,' she said, 'you'd condemn the forthcoming nuclear tests in the Pacific? As being neither good sense nor good manners?'

Meryon hesitated, for he was now treading international ground. He looked down at the microphone on the table, aware of its pointing at him, a patient ear and an accusing finger. And he chose his words.

'I think it's . . . regrettable that atmospheric tests have started again. Particularly by a nation which is a good and valued and important ally.'

Zoe grinned. 'A politic reply, Mr Meryon?'

Meryon inclined his head. 'A genuine answer.'

'You know,' Zoe went on, 'that there's a boat here in Hong Kong? Going to demonstrate against the tests? A man called Christopher Panmuir?'

'I believe I do.'

'And Panmuir can expect your support? While you yourself are in Hong Kong?'

'That's not the purpose of my visit.'

'But now that you're here,' Zoe was insistent, 'you *will* support him?'

Meryon was too experienced, Holt thought, to be caught. And indeed, Meryon's reply was neatly oblique:

'Well . . . my primary concern must be the British Public Purse. How the Navy spends *our* money.'

Napier snorted.

Meryon looked daggers at him.

Zoe turned. 'Commander Napier?'

Napier shook his head. Zoe tried Holt. 'Captain Holt,' she glanced at her notes, up again, 'you once commanded a Polaris nuclear-missile submarine?'

Holt, equally aware of the microphone, chose his words, too.

'I had that privilege.'

'Then what do atmospheric nuclear tests mean to you?'

Holt half-smiled. 'An overpowering desire to be going in the opposite direction.'

Zoe smiled back, then looked at Napier again. 'And to you, Commander?'

Napier shrugged off involvement. 'I'm only here for the cheong-sams.'

But Meryon had no intention of letting it go at that. He said easily: 'Come, Commander, don't be afraid to speak your mind.' A pause. 'I recall you're rather good at it.'

Napier realised that he was being goaded, replied levelly, 'No, sir. Unlike you, I'm not a practised public-speaker.'

Meryon was expansive. 'Then make it a private opinion.'

Zoe waited, anticipatory, enjoying the exchange. But Holt was wary. He knew nothing of a dinner at Greenwich, nothing of past exchanges; but he did know that Napier was being baited – and was in danger of being hooked.

But Napier's response was safe, if patently lame. 'I agree with Captain Holt.'

'Ha!' exclaimed Meryon.

Napier glared at him. 'Sir?'

Meryon parried the glare with a smile, then looked at Zoe.

He explained: 'The Navy has a term for it, my dear. I believe it's . . . following the senior officer's movements.'

Napier waited, now barely in control.

And then Meryon offered further explanation. 'The promotion-prospect doth make cowards of us all.'

Napier hesitated for only a fraction of a second, and then he turned to Zoe and spoke quite deliberately. 'My opinion, Miss Carter, is that if Mr Meryon had been an MP in nineteen-forty, Hitler would have stood a much better chance.'

Momentarily, Holt closed his eyes.

Meryon's eyes were glinting in triumph.

And Zoe's in delight. She asked, 'Can I quote you?'

'There is one "p" in Napier.' Napier's anger was still of the cold and dangerous kind.

But Zoe had switched off the microphone. She gathered her recording equipment, lifted her bag and stood up.

So did the men. Zoe smiled around them. 'Thank you, gentlemen. Enjoy your stay in Hong Kong.'

Meryon was smiling, too. 'I'll see you to the gangway, my dear. Thank you again for coming.'

Holt looked hard at Napier. 'And I'll show you to your cabin.'

They went out and across the flat, and to Napier's door. Napier opened it and stood aside, allowing Holt to enter.

The cabin, awaiting Napier's occupancy, was chill and bare of personal touches. And, it seemed to Napier, even chiller as Holt moved right into the cabin, to the desk, turned and gestured to Napier to close the door.

Napier did so, faced his Captain.

'I know what you're going to say, sir. But he needled me.'

'Don't you realise?' demanded Holt. 'That Carter woman was struggling. There's no real news in the sayings of Thomas Meryon, MP. He's said it all before.'

Napier waited.

'She had two lines of copy. Three at best. Until you gave her a headline. Naval Officer clashes with MP.'

'I'm sorry, sir.' Napier did not look sorry. 'But I don't like Meryon.'

'Is that relevant?'

'If he was genuine, no. But he isn't. He's simply a career-minded, publicity-hungry . . . machine.'

'Exactly,' Holt agreed. 'And this time, you gave him his publicity.'

Napier started to protest, then realised, slowly and to his horror, that Holt was right. 'I did, didn't I? The crafty old bastard! *That's* why he needled me!'

'I'd say so,' Holt nodded. 'Sit down.'

Napier sat on the bunk, while Holt hitched himself on to a corner of the desk. Holt looked at his First Lieutenant.

'James, let's put our cards on the table right away.' He paused. 'From what I've heard of you, I'm delighted to have you as second-in-command of *Hero*.'

'Thank you, sir.'

'Now,' Holt continued, 'you have a reputation for being . . . unconventional, if not outrageous.'

Napier's eyes narrowed.

'And I don't mind. Do your job and do it well, and I won't interfere.'

Napier nodded. 'Understood, sir.'

'But practise your strange beliefs to the detriment of the ship, and I'll be down on you like several tons of bricks.'

'Strange beliefs?' Napier was needled again.

'You were described to me by a senior officer ashore as . . . a rebel looking for a cause.'

Napier shrugged. 'You were described to me as Don Quixote looking for a windmill.'

There was a silence in the cabin. Holt's face was expressionless. This was, perhaps, the crunch moment in what was to become an extremely successful partnership. For, undoubtedly, Napier had gone too far for most Captains, crossed the line between friendliness and familiarity, had, indeed, been nothing short of insubordinate.

But Holt was no ordinary Captain, and not a man to shelter behind the Naval Discipline Act.

He laughed. 'You're a liar, Napier.'

Napier smiled, as much in relief as mirth. 'That's true, sir.'

Holt stood. And as Napier stood, too, Holt inspected the blue denim suit. 'I suppose . . . you do have a uniform?'

'Yes, sir. I wear it on the Queen's Birthday.'

Holt laughed again, and went out. At once, Peek knocked and came in.

'Your gear's in the flat, sir.'

'Thanks, Paul.' Napier lit a cigarette. 'Who's doing the turn-over to me?'

Peek beamed. 'I am. Acting First Lieutenant.'

'You? You couldn't turn over a new leaf, let alone a

whole department.' Napier pulled on the cigarette. 'Anyway, I've a much more important task for you. Ring up every likely hotel – Hilton, Mandarin, Repulse Bay, the lot – and try to trace a Miss Zoe Carter. Don't talk to her. Just find out where she is.'

Peek's expression was a mixture of admiration and horror. 'You aren't starting already?'

Napier was expressionless. 'To my knowledge, I've never stopped.'

The subject-to-be of Peek's search, Miss Zoe Carter, was at that moment on board a small sloop, in a yacht marina near Aberdeen village, on the south side of Hong Kong Island.

The sloop wore the red ensign and was called *Wind Song*; forty feet long, blue-hulled and with white sails which – like the canvas-dodgers on the after rails – carried the sign of the Campaign for Nuclear Disarmament. For this was Christopher Panmuir's boat and was, as Zoe had reminded Meryon, to sail into the Pacific to protest against the nuclear testing.

Panmuir intended to go single-handed. He was thirty-seven years old, dark-haired and with pale-blue eyes that had the sadness of Holt's, and a despair of their own. Yet, Panmuir was no conventional fanatic. Although it suited him to dress roughly on board *Wind Song* in casual shirt, jeans and rope-soled shoes, he was equally at home in a dark suit and a silk shirt, for he had been a successful chartered accountant in London, and held arts and economics degrees.

A bachelor and, in essence, a lonely man, Panmuir found it difficult to communicate his ideas and ideals to others, but he was strong – both mentally and physically

– and few doubted that his convictions were of matching strength.

Now, he sat opposite Zoe in the tiny cabin. He had listened to her plan without interrupting; but when she had finished, he asked, 'You think it'll work?'

'Meryon's ripe for it. You won't get a better chance.'

'Thanks, Zoe.'

'Don't thank me.' She was short with him. 'I want a story.'

'But . . . you do believe in what I'm doing? In what I'm trying to achieve?'

'People have asked me that on the streets of Saigon. And Belfast. And Beirut.'

And there was bitterness and anger in the retort. Suddenly, she was no longer the charming girl who had smiled her way through the interview with Meryon. This was a tough, tired, cynical and world-weary woman, who had seen too much and cared for too little.

'But . . . Zoe!'

'Don't saddle me with your hang-ups, Chris. I've got enough of my own.'

'All right.' Panmuir made a pacifying gesture with his hands. 'But you have to concede—'

'Save it!' She came to her feet, turned for the hatch to the upper deck. 'Give it all to Mr Thomas Meryon.'

Panmuir stood, too, but stopped to stare after her.

She turned in the hatchway.

'Come on! It's your show!'

CHAPTER THREE

KINDS OF COURAGE

In *Hero*'s Wardroom, Bill Kiley – the Weapons Electrics Officer and the elder statesman of the mess – was relaxing at the end of what he considered to be a good forenoon's work, and was reading a magazine.

The Supply Officer, Monty Wakelin, came in, crossed to the bar and started to pour himself a gin and tonic, throwing over his shoulder to Kiley: 'Is that him?'

'Who?'

'Our new Number One. Adonis in blue jeans.'

Kiley smiled. 'Don't let the outfit fool you. He's as hard as nails.'

'Oh yes?' Wakelin decided to make it a double. 'When he's not playing his guitar, you mean?'

Kiley kept the smile, said mildly: 'He does hold the George Medal, Monty. For bomb-disposal.'

'Then why dress for garbage-disposal? He's supposed to be a Naval Officer, not a walking advert for Wranglers.'

'You'll get used to him,' Kiley soothed. 'When he was in *Decoy*, he—'

The door opened again and Napier, now in uniform shirt and shorts, entered and grinned to the two officers.

'Morning, gentlemen.' And to Kiley, holding out his hand. 'Bill, long time.'

'Hello, James.' Kiley gestured to Wakelin. 'Monty Wakelin, the Pusser.'

Napier and Wakelin shook hands. And Wakelin offered an olive branch.

'What will you have, sir? Gin and tonic?'

Napier lifted an eyebrow. 'Is the bar open?'

'In *Hero*,' Wakelin assured him, 'the bar never closes!'

Napier said pleasantly, 'Well, close it now. You can open it again at midday – in accordance with Captain's Standing Orders.'

Wakelin stared. 'But . . . it's ten to twelve!'

'Then,' another smile from Napier, 'you haven't long to wait.' He turned to Kiley. 'Bill, if you'd look in on me sometime?'

'I'll be there.'

'Thanks.'

Napier embraced them both in yet another smile, turned and left the mess. There was a silence – until the struggling Wakelin found his voice again.

'Who the hell does he think he is?'

'He thinks he's the First Lieutenant,' Kiley answered, secretly delighted. 'And he's got an appointment to prove it.'

Meryon must have been surprised when Peek knocked on his door, to announce the presence of Zoe and Panmuir. But it was as if the politician had been waiting all forenoon for the honour of their calling, and he ushered them into the night-cabin with a great display of warmth and enthusiasm.

Panmuir, suddenly awkward in the gale of Meryon's effusiveness, managed, 'Good of you to see us, sir.'

'Not at all,' Meryon told him. 'A great pleasure to meet you.' He positively beamed at them. 'Please sit down.'

Zoe and Panmuir found chairs and Meryon perched himself on the bunk, beamed anew.

'Now what can I do for you?'

Panmuir licked his lips. 'I've come to ask, sir, if you'll speak on behalf of the *Wind Song* project.'

'*Wind Song*?' queried Meryon.

Panmuir's face fell. 'Oh . . . I . . . Zoe said you knew about my work. *Wind Song*'s my boat and—'

'Yes, of course!' Meryon waved an apologetic hand. 'I know all about your work. I commend it.'

'Then will you speak? At a press conference?'

It was Meryon's turn to hesitate.

'What would you want me to say?'

Panmuir was genuinely surprised. 'Well . . . to condemn atmospheric nuclear testing. To call for this series of tests in the Pacific to be abandoned, scrapped. To . . . to endorse what I intend to do in *Wind Song*.'

'Which is?'

'Sail for the test area. Send radio bulletins to the world. Cause embarrassment. Stir up feeling against the tests.'

Meryon frowned. 'People tried that in seventy-two and seventy-three. What was it called . . . Greenpeace?'

'Yes,' Panmuir nodded. 'A man called McTaggart in a ketch called *Vega*.'

'And now,' Meryon said pointedly, 'it's a man called Panmuir in a boat called *Wind Song*?'

'With, if you'll help,' Panmuir was earnest, appealing, 'the voice of an English politician. A strong voice.'

'Thank you.' Meryon sighed, dramatically. 'The problem is . . . I *am* a politician. With a party loyalty. And this whole business has . . . international ramifications.'

'Yes!' Panmuir's jaw went out. 'Which means that there should be international protest! Outcry world-wide!' He sighed, too, shook his head. 'But no-one gives a damn.'

Meryon leaned forward. 'Oh, I do. I assure you. But . . .'

He shrugged expressively.

And Zoe spoke for the first time, throwing the line away, underplaying her hand. 'We understand,' she said. 'You could be rapped if your face suddenly appeared on the cover of *Newsweek*.'

Meryon's eyes glinted momentarily, but he was too cautious to make a frontal attack. He looked to Zoe, threw back as casually. 'You think you could get coverage for *Wind Song*?'

'I'll get it. Pity is . . . I could get a lot more if it was known as the Meryon-Panmuir project.'

Meryon scratched at his nose, perhaps to hide his expression. 'I'm not the Prime Minister, you know.'

'But you *are* a name.' Zoe was still operating in low key. 'With a good track record for work on disarmament.'

Meryon was humble. 'All the same, you may be over-assessing my influence.'

'Well . . . we *would* need an angle.' And still, Zoe was not pushing it; but speaking more with sincerity than emphasis. 'And I think I've got one.' She paused, causing Meryon to lean forward again in impatience. 'We've got to hang it on courage – two men against a nation.'

Meryon's eyes were now alight; but he, too, could play it down. He nodded slowly, conceding: 'Yes . . . I like that.'

'Chris's courage,' Zoe went on, glancing at Panmuir, 'is obvious, the physical kind. And yours has to be moral courage, fearlessness of . . . of environment and convention.'

Meryon was clearly taken with the image. Yet, even now, he was giving little away.

'Go on.'

'This is a warship, a weapon of war. Just as nuclear bombs are weapons of war. A ship commanded by an ex-Polaris captain – a man who accepts that nuclear warfare is at least a possibility.'

'Yes . . . ?'

Zoe dropped her own bombshell. 'Hold the press conference in HMS *Hero.*'

'In *Hero*?' Meryon was appalled.

'That's what it needs,' Zoe said, starting deliberately to talk in headlines. 'A dove among the hawks. A man with the courage to conduct his crusade for peace from within . . . would you forgive "the very lair of the warmongers"?'

'No.' Meryon sounded disappointed. 'They'd never allow it. Captain Holt would never give permission.'

Zoe shrugged. 'Don't ask him.'

'I must!'

'Why?' Zoe was challenging now. 'If I can use your name, I'll alert the other correspondents, have it announced on local radio and TV tonight. Press conference, HMS *Hero*, eleven o'clock tomorrow morning.'

Meryon looked doubtful.

Zoe pressed on. 'When it's fait accompli, what can he do?'

'Refuse to let the Press on board.'

'And be accused of gagging an MP? Frustrating the cause of peace?' She shook her head. 'Too embarrassing for them.'

But still, Meryon hesitated. Encouragingly, Zoe said, 'Come on, Mr Meryon! You've fought the Navy too long to worry about their susceptibilities now!'

'Yes . . . but this is . . . underhand.'

'So is nuclear testing,' she reminded him. 'And that's what concerns us.'

And Panmuir looked sharply at Zoe, and frowned.

But Zoe was pleading to Meryon, as if totally committed.

Holt and Napier were talking together on the flight deck when Zoe and Panmuir appeared from the waist and made for the gangway. Zoe smiled to the two officers.

'Captain Holt, Commander.'

Holt returned the smile. 'Miss Carter.'

He and Napier saluted Zoe and Panmuir over the side; and then he looked to where Peek was standing near the quartermaster's desk.

'Paul.'

Peek approached his Captain. 'Sir?'

'Have you got the duty now?'

'Yes, sir.'

'Any idea how Miss Carter and her friend got on board?'

A flicker of concern on Peek's face. 'They asked for Mr Meryon, sir. I thought . . .'

'Yes, all right.' Holt nodded, dismissively. Then as Peek turned away: 'Oh – do we know who the gentleman is?'

'A Mr . . . Panmuir, sir.'

Holt frowned. 'I see.'

He looked down to the jetty, to where Zoe and Panmuir were walking away. And frowned again.

Panmuir was frowning, too. 'Zoe . . . ?'

'Yes?'

'You aren't being devious, are you?'

She glanced at him. 'In what way?'

'The prose was a bit purple back there. "Dove among the hawks" and all that.'

'Always tell them what they want to hear.'

'But you were selling it very hard. And not for *Wind Song.*'

'No,' she confessed easily. 'For a story.'

Panmuir stopped to look at her. She stopped with him.

He grimaced, said, 'I wish I could get inside that mind of yours.'

Zoe smiled. 'You'd never find your way around.'

And she walked on.

From the flight deck, Holt watched them out of sight, then turned – troubled – to Napier.

'I wonder what all that was about?'

'Panmuir's the ban-the-bomb merchant?'

'Yes.' Holt considered. 'Shall we seek an audience, too?'

'With His Excellency,' Napier grinned, 'the Prince of Politics?'

'Careful, James,' admonished Holt. 'Your true-blue blood could make a mess of the paintwork.'

He led the way up the waist.

They encountered Meryon in the cabin flat and, for once, Meryon's guard slipped and – to Holt's increasing concern – he looked nothing less than furtive.

Holt asked, 'Could we have a word, Mr Meryon?'

'Ah, of course.'

Holt indicated the door to the day-cabin and all three passed inside.

Holt met Meryon's gaze, held it. 'What was Panmuir doing on board?'

'He came to see me.'

'Why?'

Meryon shrugged. 'He wants me to support the *Wind Song* project.'

'And?'

'I agreed.'

'Mr Meryon,' Holt was controlled, but firm, 'I would prefer that you didn't use HMS *Hero* as a base for that kind of activity.'

Meryon hesitated. 'What kind of activity?'

'Panmuir does not enjoy the support of the Government. Your Government and mine.'

'So?'

'So – if you're active on his behalf while you're living in the ship, it could raise all kinds of questions for the outside world. And reflect on me, the Naval Base here, the Ministry of Defence . . .'

'I'll make clear,' Meryon was uncomfortable, 'that everything I do is from a . . . a personal standpoint.'

'What you make clear,' Holt returned patiently, 'and what is reported could be – as you well know – two entirely different things.'

Meryon could have chosen defiance; instead, he elected to try an open, frank approach.

'Oh, dear. Then I may have offended already.'

Holt's heart sank. 'Yes?'

'I've agreed to give a press conference at eleven o'clock tomorrow morning.'

Holt's heart sank still further.

'Where?'

Meryon affected surprise. 'Well . . . here, of course.'

Holt stared at him. 'Here? In the ship?'

'I was sure you wouldn't object.'

'It's not a question of objection, Mr Meryon. But one of courtesy.'

'Courtesy?'

'You are a guest in this ship. And in this ship, nothing happens without my permission.' A pause. 'My prior permission.'

Meryon adopted his pose of humbleness. 'I apologise. Sincerely.'

'I must ask you to cancel your conference.'

'Ah.' Now, Meryon managed a doleful countenance. 'That would be . . . embarrassing.'

'To whom?' Holt was coldly angry.

'All of us, I'm afraid.' Meryon shook his head in sorrow. 'It could be taken the wrong way . . . that the Navy's trying to muzzle an anti-nuclear protest.'

Holt's heart plummeted to somewhere in the region of his buckskin shoes.

'You've announced it already?'

'Yes. Notices to TV, radio, all the correspondents.'

Holt thought quickly. He could arrange still for the conference to be cancelled, but there was no doubt that Meryon would capitalise on the cancellation and escalate it into an issue of the Navy against the pacifists. Thus, there was less mileage in it if he allowed the conference to go ahead, as simply yet another speech from Thomas Albert Meryon.

And he could offload the whole thing on Captain-in-Charge ashore. Let him sort out Meryon. But the fact remained that it was *Hero*'s Officer of the Day who had failed to intercept Panmuir, had failed to report Panmuir's presence on board to Holt or Napier, had not thought to insist that a ship's officer attended the discussion in the night-cabin.

It was *Hero*'s fault; and thus, it was Holt's own problem.

He looked to Napier. 'James, get on to the Joint Services PRO ashore, warn him. And tell the main gate that we'll be getting reporters in about eleven tomorrow morning.'

'Aye aye, sir.' Napier started to go, then turned back to Meryon. 'May I ask, sir, what the theme of tomorrow's dissertation will be?'

Meryon tried a sad smile. 'The state of the world, Commander. What else?'

Napier glared at him, started again to leave.

Holt said quietly, 'Close the door, James.'

Napier left, closing the door. Holt waited until it was firmly shut, then stared at Meryon for a very long moment. And when he spoke, his voice was controlled. Not once did he raise it, but the words slammed into Meryon like physical blows.

'You may think that you've been desperately clever. But let me assure you that you are still in this ship only because I prize certain old-fashioned values. While you are my guest, I must accommodate you, your idiosyncrasies and your incivilities. Let me make clear, however, that should you try to be clever again, you will find yourself sitting on your backside on the jetty, with all your possessions and your pomposity around you.'

Holt strode from the cabin, leaving a very sober and very thoughtful politician.

CHAPTER FOUR

DON QUIXOTE

By seven o'clock that evening, Napier had unpacked, bathed and changed into a lightweight grey suit, and Peek, in white mess undress, met him in the cabin flat with Zoe Carter's telephone number.

'Excelsior Hotel,' Peek reported, with an air of triumph. 'Room two-double-one-seven.'

Napier took the telephone number (written on the back of a bar-chit) from Peek, bore it reverently across the flat and lifted the shore telephone, dialling the operator.

Into the telephone, he said: 'Hong Kong seven-six-seven-three-six-five, please.'

Peek made no move to leave, but enquired decently, 'Mind if I stay and watch?'

Napier grinned. 'Now or later?' And into the 'phone: 'Room two-double-one-seven, please.'

Peek leaned on the bulkhead, to enjoy the show, as Napier launched into his campaign.

'Miss Carter? Hello, it's James Napier, from HMS *Hero*.' A pause. 'Look . . . I . . . well, I had this very fine speech rehearsed, but . . . I'm no good with girls . . . and I just wanted to ask if you'll have dinner with me.'

He listened. 'I see.' Then: 'Yes, of course. Bye.'

He hung up, looked to Peek. 'She loves me.'

Peek scoffed. 'Oh yes? What did she say?'

'She wants to write my life-story,' boasted Napier. 'Posthumously.'

'What?'

'She told me to drop dead.'

'Tough.' Peek was privately pleased: it was a comfort to him to know that even James Napier could fail; for, contrary to expectations (and, incidentally, Peek's claims in the Wardroom), he had himself failed throughout the Far East tour and, were he honest, had not fared much better in the United Kingdom.

'Well,' Peek said brightly, 'that's that.'

'It isn't.' Napier was moving back to his cabin. 'I've got an old address-book somewhere.'

He stopped, glanced back at Holt's day-cabin. 'Reckon Father's got a likely list tucked away?'

'No.' Peek shook his head with complete conviction. 'I haven't seen Father with a bird since he joined. He's a bit of a loner.'

And it was true that Holt was alone. As it was true, in general, that he preferred his own company ashore. On occasions, of course, he did run-ashore with his officers, the better to know them; but he was no great drinker, and he enjoyed his solitary dinners in foreign ports as a time to contemplate, to reflect and to observe.

Now, he was in the market in Aberdeen village, walking among the open-air stalls and enjoying all the hustle and bustle and colour and cacophony around him. He wandered aimlessly, his eyes dancing across the displays of cheap T-shirts, toys, fruit, vegetables, cooked foods and home-made sandals. No-one pressed him to buy; no-one challenged his right to meander where he willed.

He wore a two-piece suit, with the jacket slung over one shoulder, sunglasses against the glare in the evening sky, a smile to the sheer joy of escape.

Zoe's voice jerked him from his thoughts. 'Penny for them, Captain?'

He turned, stared, then smiled again, removing the glasses. 'Miss Carter. Forgive me. For a moment, I didn't recognise you.'

'Out of uniform, you mean?' she grinned.

And out of uniform was right. Gone were the shirt and slacks. She was dressed now in a short blue evening dress, with a lightweight matching cape; her hair was carefully composed; the tough little reporter was all at once a very sophisticated and strikingly attractive woman.

She asked, 'What's the allurement of Aberdeen village?'

'Oh . . . peace, quiet.'

Zoe cast a glance around her, at the mêlée of humanity. 'Oh yes?'

Holt explained: 'It's on the other side of the island from my ship.' And with another smile: 'What's your excuse?'

'Much the same, I suppose.'

They had started to walk on. Holt looked sideways to her.

'Do I have you to blame for tomorrow's press conference?'

She parried that one. 'I'm out of uniform, remember? Off duty.'

'All right,' he half-smiled. 'But I've a suspicion that I should auction your head in this market.'

Zoe looked back at him, hesitated, then made a conscious decision.

'Okay, I'll make reparation. What are you doing for dinner?'

Holt started in surprise. 'What am I . . .?'

'Come on. I'll buy you a lump of fish on a floating restaurant.'

'But . . . I can't let *you* buy *me* dinner. If you'll allow me . . .'

'I accept,' Zoe said firmly. And laughed: 'What a nice idea of yours!'

The floating restaurants in Aberdeen harbour are world-famous tourist-attractions, for which very good reason Holt had always avoided them. But Zoe assured him that the Tai Pak was to be recommended, in terms of both comfort and cuisine, and thus he permitted himself to be steered by her to the sampan jetties.

To Holt, the harbour at Aberdeen was nothing less than incredible. Within its relatively tiny water-space, some twenty-thousand people existed, living on no more than three-thousand sampans – the smallest of which could not have housed a fair-sized dog without, in England, a howl of anguish from the RSPCA.

Undeniably, the smells were an assault on the European nose, but, as Holt knew, it was a sight unique in the world, and there was in the people of Aberdeen a cheerful and enduring courage that never failed to touch him.

Zoe and he took a sampan from the Tai Pak jetty to the restaurant. The boat was poled by a mother and daughter: the mother in wide straw hat and black, loose-fitting trouser-suit, the daughter in bright red shirt and blue jeans. Clearly, the bread-winner had died – but, Holt thought, that was no excuse for them: the boat was poled and – somehow – a living was made.

He looked to Zoe, smiled. 'Do you envy them their life afloat?'

'No way.' She shook her head emphatically. 'I like

my water hot and cold.'

'Yes . . . but there *is* something simple and . . . uncomplicated about it all.'

'As long as they live,' Zoe rejoined realistically. And then: 'Suppose it would be a daft question to ask how you feel about boats?'

'Boats to me,' he said, 'means submarines. And those were my life.'

'Ah yes. You must tell me what it's like in a Polaris.'

He lifted an eyebrow, answered in mock-seriousness: 'I'm out of uniform. Off-duty.'

And she laughed again.

The sampan came alongside the floating restaurant and Holt paid the older woman and helped Zoe out of the boat and on to the Tai Pak. They passed inside and into the main restaurant, a long oblong hall with white-covered tables arranged neatly and spaced well apart. They were early and the place was less than half-full.

Holt's spirits lifted as they were shown to a table and given menus. He had forgotten that he had promised himself one of his solitary dinners, and he looked at the girl across the table with contentment, and a sudden anxiety to please her.

'I hope you're hungry.'

'Hungry enough,' Zoe assured him, 'to cope with . . . shark's fin soup, steamed fish and a bottle or six of the local firewater.'

Holt felt awkward. 'Would it offend you if I stay on soft drinks?'

'I'm not going to seduce you, Captain.'

'It's Edward. And I'm not very clever at drinking.'

To his own ears, it sounded like an admission of a lack of virility. But Zoe smiled.

'All it takes is practice.'

'Then perhaps I'll have a brandy with my coffee.'

Zoe smiled again. 'With Meryon on board, I'm surprised you haven't been driven to the bottle.'

'Oh,' Holt said, considering, 'perhaps his heart is in the right place.'

'What?' Zoe was amazed.

He shrugged. 'Can't condemn a man entirely because ... his opinions conflict with your own.'

'But Meryon,' she protested, 'has never had an opinion. Not an original one. Everything he utters or does is strictly for public consumption.'

'Well, maybe that could be said of all of us.'

Zoe smiled in wonder, shook her head. '"Where do you see all the good that you see ...?"'

'Mmm?'

'Man of La Mancha.'

'Who?'

'Don Quixote.'

'Oh!' He laughed. 'You've been talking to my new First Lieutenant. He thinks I was born on a white charger.'

'He could be right.'

'Don't you believe it.'

Zoe looked at him, shook her head again. 'I bet you're kind to children and old ladies, and your home's full of dogs, cats and goldfish.'

'My home's a cabin in *Hero*.' He smiled. 'With not even a parrot in sight.'

'But ... in England?'

'I'm divorced,' he returned flatly.

But it hurt. Still. For, even now, he could see it only as a failure. And it hurt the more because it was his only real failure. Professionally, life had been a success; personally, it had been a disaster.

Yet now, he managed to grin to Zoe. He said: 'She's married again. Another Naval Officer.' And, keeping the grin: 'Some people never learn.'

The same could have been said that evening of James Napier: when Peek returned from evening rounds, Napier was again in the cabin flat and again on the telephone.

Before him was his old, dog-eared and well-used address-book. Once, it had been the envy of the Far East Fleet, but now it was serving him with rather less than its former distinction.

Already, it had given Napier two husbands (one suspicious and the other irate), a polite but somewhat one-side conversation in Cantonese, a garage and an 'unobtainable' signal. But he was nothing if not steadfast. And perseverance was ultimately rewarded: he found himself talking to a girl whom he had known – and quite well – in the *Decoy* days.

'Mary!' The charm hit full-strength in the one word. 'It's James Napier.'

A pause. 'James . . . Napier.'

Peek grinned as Napier admitted to the telephone: 'Yes, it has been a long time. I've just arrived back in Hong Kong. This evening. And naturally, you were my first thought.' He winked at Peek. 'I wondered about dinner tonight? Or a drink later on?'

A much longer pause.

'Oh, what a shame. Yes . . . don't drown yourself.'

He replaced the receiver, explained to Peek with a grimace, 'Washing her hair.' He sighed. 'There was a time when the birds on this Island were reliable.'

Peek was hopeful. 'We *could* start on the turn-over.'

'I'm not spending my first night in Hong Kong mustering Naval stores.'

'Haven't you got jet-lag?'

'And brewer's droop, for all I know.' Napier grimaced again. 'I'd simply like the chance to find out!'

Darkness had fallen at Aberdeen, and the Tai Pak was a blaze of multi-coloured lights.

Zoe and Holt were finishing the main course, and Zoe was on her second bottle of local wine. Holt was sticking doggedly to coke.

It amused Zoe.

'I don't suppose you smoke, either?'

'No,' he confessed. 'I don't.'

Once, he had smoked. And heavily. But he had stopped on the day on which the elder of his two daughters had been born; for it had seemed to him then that he should not take unnecessary risks with his health, lest he leave the child fatherless. Even at the time, he was aware that the gesture was perhaps over-dramatic, and the measure over-drastic, but in another way, he felt that it was a duty – and duty and loyalty had ruled much of Holt's life.

The unbidden thought of his daughters had sent a flicker of sadness across his face, and Zoe read it.

She asked, 'Are you happy?'

The question took Holt by surprise. He smiled to cover his confusion, said, 'You're off-duty. Remember?'

'A purely private enquiry.'

'Very well,' he searched for a word. 'I'm . . . un-troubled.'

It was lie, but it was also an answer. And to kill the line of query, he turned it back on her.

'And you?'

'I get along,' she said.

'You've never married?'

Zoe looked at him. 'Is that synonymous with happiness?'

'No . . . but you're an attractive girl. Intelligent, amusing—'

'If you say so,' she cut in; and her voice was suddenly flat.

Holt offered quietly: 'Don't undersell yourself.'

'And don't waste your time.'

'Sorry?'

Zoe put down her glass, met his eyes. 'Edward, I've had enough lines to start a railway network.' Now, her voice was tired. 'Tonight, I'm going to have one coffee and one liqueur. Then we'll share a taxi as far as my hotel. Where we'll say goodbye.'

Holt's own voice was carefully even, despite his bafflement (and alarm) at her inexplicable change of mood. He said: 'My plans are no different.'

She stared at him, her face expressionless, her eyes registering only cynicism. Then, at length: 'No . . . perhaps not. I apologise.'

'Except,' Holt took up his theme again, 'that I hope it will be "goodnight" at the hotel. And not "goodbye".' He smiled to her. 'I've enjoyed this evening.'

'I'm glad.' She did not return the smile.

'I hope we'll meet again.'

'We shall.'

'Tomorrow?' Tentatively.

She nodded. 'Tomorrow morning. Eleven o'clock.' And, with defiance: 'At the Press Conference.'

They did share a taxi to the Excelsior, Zoe's hotel, but

there, Holt paid it off, electing to walk back to the Naval Base.

His leave-taking of Zoe was almost formal, and oddly uncomfortable. On the hotel steps, she held out her hand – as she had done when they first met – and, feeling slightly foolish beneath the scrutiny of the Sikh doorman, Holt took the hand and said: 'Goodnight, Zoe.'

'Goodnight, Edward. Thanks for dinner.'

And she turned, and was gone.

Holt walked away, wondering why it should matter that the evening had been unsatisfactory; and, most of all, wondering why the girl should have touched some forgotten chord. On the surface, she was a hard and uncompromising bitch, nothing less. But occasionally, fleetingly, there had been a glimpse of another dimension; a suggestion of defencelessness beneath the barrier of cynicism . . . and perhaps, too, old wounds that still bled.

It did not occur to him then, of course, that he could see in her much of himself, and of his own problems. And he could not understand why he should recognise so readily that strange compendium of independence and vulnerability. He knew only that the desire to see her again was genuine; and that, in itself, was remarkable: there had been no desire in his life since Laura.

The former Mrs Holt.

The ex-wife.

Ex-lover.

Ex.

He walked on, down Gloucester Road, lost in his thoughts – until he came to the China Fleet Club. Here, Pat Fuller and Leading Seaman Hans Anderson were making the long trek from doorway to kerbside, and concentrating hard on steering a steady course.

Anderson, nonetheless, spotted his Captain, saluted and grinned: 'Good run, sir?'

'Not bad, Anderson. And yourself?'

'Been teaching the Leading Reg how to drink.'

'Rubbish,' commented Fuller. And to Holt: 'Want to share a cab, sir?'

Holt watched as Fuller waved at a passing taxi, and almost fell over with the effort. The taxi, perhaps interpreting Fuller's gesture as belligerence, went on past.

'Well,' Holt concluded doubtfully, 'if you can get one.'

'Easy,' Anderson assured him, indicating that Holt should continue to observe Fuller and enjoy the work of a maestro.

And indeed, at the very next attempt, Fuller did obtain the services of a large red cab – by the simple expedient of stepping into the middle of the road and causing it to screech to a heart-lurching stop.

'If he tries that,' Holt warned mildly, 'when we go to Tokyo, he won't live to pay the fare.'

'Oh, it's all right, sir.' Anderson nodded sagely. 'He can judge it to the second – but only when he's pissed.' And then in hasty and quite unnecessary amendment: 'Beg pardon, sir . . . when he's smashed.'

Holt glanced again at Fuller.

'Looks pissed to me,' he decided.

Anderson laughed, held open the cab door for Holt.

CHAPTER FIVE

NIGHT-THOUGHTS

In her room on the twenty-first floor of the Excelsior Hotel, Zoe Carter sat by the picture-window and looked out on the night-panorama of Hong Kong harbour.

The window was, in fact, one of the best-possible vantage points for one of the most remarkable views in the world: if Hong Kong is breathtaking by day, it is stunning by night.

The mountains rise black against a dark-blue sky. The senses are mesmerised by the millions of coloured lights, from buildings, streets, ships – even the winking fireflies of aircraft, on the runway at Kai Tak. The water mirrors all, doubling the effect, intensifying the images, beguiling the eyes.

In all the world, only Rio de Janiero and San Francisco can rival it, but they lack that indefinable ingredient which is the magic of the Orient, the mystery of the East, the promise of an enchanted land. Even in the hotel room, high above Causeway Bay and divorced from the sounds and smells of a city still throbbing with life, it should have been impossible not to be moved by the sheer grandeur of it.

But Zoe barely saw it. She was preparing her questions for the Press Conference.

And planning.

Planning the downfall of Thomas Albert Meryon.

Meryon paced the night-cabin, in gold pyjamas and red

dressing-gown, and rehearsed his speech for the morrow.

The words were easy: he had an almost photographic memory and spoke always – and impressively – without notes. But the key to delivery was in pause, gesture and tone, in the catch of the voice, the shake of the head, the emphasis of the clenched fist. And these were the things which required painstaking rehearsal, to ensure that they appeared to be both spontaneous and natural.

Meryon had no illusions about what he was doing: he believed simply that it was part of his job to manipulate the minds of those less gifted; to lead, that others might follow; to gather about him a great army, a faithful host to whom the name of Meryon was synonymous with hope; to become, ultimately, the voice of the people and the inspiration of the party.

And there was every chance that he would achieve his aim. For he had plotted every move, weighed every factor, tested every rung on his own personal ladder to success. While others climbed the political mountain by conventional means, taking short-cuts where they could and stepping by right on the bodies of those who faltered, he had remained steadfastly on his own tortuous trail. While other sought jobs in Government, sold their souls for favours, secured less-talented men as patrons and protectors, he had waited. And grown stronger.

He had kept his armour bright, untarnished by the dirt and the blood of internal power-struggles. He had cultivated the media, and allowed it always to be known that any fees resulting from his many radio and TV appearances were sent to charity. He had learned to campaign by barnstorming, by getting into the streets and meeting the people, by going down mines and on to the factory floors.

For one day, the call could come. Would come, he

was sure. And he would step from the wings, and assume the mantle of greatness.

And it could be done.

For he had planned for that very day.

All his life.

In the cabin of *Wind Song*, in the least uncomfortable of the two narrow bunks, Christopher Panmuir lay listening to the slap of water on the boat's hull, and thinking of the Press conference on the morrow.

It would be a help, in that Meryon was column-space in newspapers. And for that, he was grateful. But it would not be an answer; it would not cause an upsurge of horror and indignation across the world – or even across Hong Kong. For nothing, he knew in his heart, would take the world by the throat and send it clamouring to the anti-nuclear banner. If the world ran true to form, indeed, nothing would happen at all.

How many denizens of this dismal and polluted planet remembered David McTaggart, Nigel Ingram, Grant Davidson, Mary Lornie, Anne-Marie Horne?

Who spoke today of *Greenpeace* III?

Who recalled the voyages of *Vega* in 1972 and 1973?

Who cared that the French had rammed *Vega* in 1972, and had boarded and beaten up McTaggart and Ingram in 1973?

Who could take a map and mark the position of Mururoa Atoll?

Who could explain the real differences between atmospheric and underground tests, and their respective hazards?

Who gave a damn, anyway, about any kind of nuclear-testing in the far-off Pacific?

And what could he do?

What could anyone do?

Why was Zoe Carter suddenly involved?

Panmuir shifted in the bunk to this new thought, frowned to the darkness.

That was a point – what the hell *was* Zoe doing?

He knew very little about her. At first, when she had appeared on the jetty one forenoon and offered conversation, he had thought that she was merely some freak, akin to the groupies who hang around pop groups, come to see the man who was to send himself on a trip – both literally and figuratively – against a nuclear bomb.

And even when he had discovered who she was, and what she wanted, he had learned no more. She had refused to dine with him, while offering readily to help prepare the boat. She had refused to talk about his beliefs, except insomuch as they affected her material for newscopy.

So. What was she doing now?

If she wanted a story – and he could not believe that she had any higher motive – why was she sharing the great day with every other correspondent and reporter whom she could muster? Why had she bothered to arrange the Press conference in the first place?

She had cultivated himself; and then Meryon. Thus, she had been a lap ahead of the field on the *Wind Song* story . . . and now, deliberately, she was throwing away that advantage?

He changed position again, groping for cigarettes and matches.

Zoe was using him.

The problem was, he could not see how.

Or why.

CHAPTER SIX

COUNTER-CHALLENGE

'And I believe,' Meryon asserted, his voice tripping to the emotion of his belief, 'that any nation which attempts to close off one hundred thousand square miles of sea should be challenged.' He paused, one of his planned pauses. 'But a nation which does that for nuclear testing and the propagation of nuclear weaponry should be actively opposed.'

Holt grimaced. They were in the wardroom of *Hero*, which had been rigged and re-arranged for the Press Conference, and it was standing-room only. There were television cameras, radio microphones, extra lighting, cables everywhere. There were reporters and photographers and feature-writers.

And there was Meryon.

He stood behind a small table at the after end of the wardroom, facing his audience, projecting a relaxed and reasoned approach. But he was nonetheless totally in control of the gathering.

Close to him, on one side, Holt and Napier sat and listened in anxiety as denouncements of armed force and military strength rang around the bulkheads in the officers' mess of a warship.

On Meryon's other side, Panmuir was motionless and expressionless.

In the front row of the reporters, Zoe sat quietly, a half-smile playing on her lips.

'The *Wind Song* project,' Meryon continued, 'is providing just that. Active opposition. And I laud and applaud Mr Panmuir as a champion of the cause of peace.'

He nodded to Panmuir, then looked up and around the gathering, his face shining in sincerity, his jaw set in conviction.

And for the first time, Zoe came to her feet.

Panmuir, for the first time, showed expression: a mixture of alarm and mistrust.

But Zoe was smiling: 'Would you say, Mr Meryon, that this is a case where actions must speak louder than words?'

Meryon nodded again, said with gravity: 'Indeed, I would.'

'Then why,' Zoe kept her smile, 'don't you sail in *Wind Song*?'

There was a gasp around the wardroom. Then silence, as breaths were held, hanging on Meryon's reply.

Meryon was stunned. 'I . . . I beg your pardon?'

'Why,' Zoe repeated patiently, 'don't you sail in *Wind Song* – help Mr Panmuir oppose the tests?'

Meryon saw the trap. And he smiled back at Zoe, a sympathetic smile, as one might use to favour an idiot or a backward child.

'My dear Miss Carter, I wish that I could. But each of us has a part to play in the scheme of things. Christopher Panmuir will make the voyage. I shall remain at base, as it were, and ensure that the world does not overlook his bravery.'

Zoe shook her head, sighed audibly. 'Isn't that rather like a priest at confessional? The pleasures and the risks are all vicarious.'

There was a titter of laughter from the reporters. Meryon's face went cold.

'It was Milton, I believe, who said "they also serve

who only stand and wait". And sometimes, that is the harder thing to do.'

Zoe shrugged. 'It was Lady Macduff, I believe, who said "our fears do make us traitors". And she wasn't wrong.'

Now, Panmuir's face betrayed horror at what Zoe was doing. And Holt's face was set in concern. He had hoped for the minimum reaction to the *Hero* conference – and there was no way now that this would not hit headlines across the world.

'Dear girl,' Meryon was condescending, 'you may not have grasped that, as a Member of Parliament, I am not free to obey the bidding of my heart. Not in matters with such clear political and international considerations.'

'Then resign,' countered Zoe. 'Or is your monthly pay-cheque more important than your principles?'

Meryon looked around the assembly again, in apology for Zoe's interruption. Then, conversationally and with an air of long-suffering, he queried: 'Young lady, why are you so objectionable?'

'Because,' Zoe retorted fiercely, 'you've been allowed to get away with it for years. You've stood up at meetings all over the place, and told us how wonderful you are, what a campaigner you are, how self-sacrificing you are.' Her lips curled. 'Well, Mr Meryon, stand up again now. And be counted.'

'I *am* standing, Miss Carter.' He smiled, but the smile did not reach his eyes. 'And trying patiently to establish your reasons for this ridiculous line of questioning. What exactly *is* your interest?'

'Not a lot.' Zoe was deliberately, stingingly contemptuous. 'Just a morbid curiosity to know how you'll talk your way out of this one. Because I'm sure you can, Mr Meryon – you're so good at *talking.*'

And Meryon had lost.

He knew it, could see it in the eyes of the reporters, could feel it in the atmosphere around the room. And a dream was slipping from his grasp. This girl had hurled mud at the polished armour, and some of that mud would stick. She had challenged his credibility, and without credibility, his day would never come.

He looked to Panmuir, whose head was bowed. And he looked to Holt and thought that he could read sympathy in the Captain's eyes.

Then he looked at his audience, and he lifted his voice.

'Very well, Miss Carter. If Mr Panmuir will have me, I shall sail in *Wind Song.*' And he looked directly at the smiling Zoe. 'Provided that you sail, too, to report the voyage.'

There was a gasp from the reporters, and Zoe's smile tilted. But there was nothing that she could do about it: she had accused Meryon of being afraid, and if she backed away now, he might use her retreat to wriggle himself out.

It was a clever trick, and a vicious one. But she, too, had been clever and vicious, and she had never underestimated Meryon's ability to fight in this kind of arena.

With an effort, she widened her smile. 'I wouldn't miss it for the world.'

And she sat, and left Meryon to quell the uproar, and conclude the meeting.

Panmuir caught up with Zoe in the cabin flat, fighting his way through a mêlée of departing reporters and equipment, to get at her.

And he was angry.

'You conned us both! Meryon and me!'

Zoe attacked in turn. 'What are you talking about? Meryon wanted billing as the courageous crusader. He's got it. You wanted *Wind Song* on the front page. You've got that, too.'

'I won't take Meryon!'

'Don't be a fool!' Zoe's eyes were blazing. 'If you go on your own, you'll be forgotten in two days. But Meryon will keep the Press interested. Especially after this row. I've done you a big favour, Chris, so why don't you just say thanks and clear off!'

'Why?'

'Why what?'

'Why did you do it? The others have got the story, too.'

'But I've got the first-hand story,' Zoe said, in satisfaction. 'I'm the gal who put the screws on Meryon.'

Panmuir grimaced. 'Yes . . . did you *have* to do it that way?'

'Too right!' Zoe was fierce again. 'Meryon's a windbag, and he always has been. All I did was stick a pin in him!'

Panmuir stared at her, shook his head and turned away, for the port screen door.

Zoe, wisely, turned for the starboard door instead – but walked immediately into Holt, who had clearly heard every word of her exchange with Panmuir, in his cabin doorway.

Holt said flatly: 'Come in.'

She hesitated, then went into the cabin. Holt closed the door behind her, turned from it and faced her.

Zoe waited, standing in the middle of the cabin.

Quietly, Holt ordered: 'Sit down.'

'Don't give me instructions, Captain. I'm not your cabin-boy.'

Holt's voice stayed quiet. 'Sit . . . down.'

She hesitated again, then shrugged, sighed and went to sit in an armchair.

Holt remained standing, and staring. 'I hope you're proud of yourself.'

'Pride,' she countered evenly, 'is a luxury I can't afford.'

'As Panmuir said, you conned Meryon. And manoeuvred him into possible danger.'

'What danger?'

'*Wind Song* is going to the test-area.'

Zoe shrugged again. 'So what? Panmuir's not going to get himself fried for his cause. And sure as hell, Thomas Meryon isn't!'

'And you?' Holt asked. 'What does *Wind Song* really mean to you?'

She laughed, shortly and bitterly.

'I'm not paid to change the world.'

He looked at her for a long moment, then crossed the cabin to the starboard-side scuttle, and stared out. He spoke without turning back to her, his thoughts half-formed.

'We're each of us on his own road, Zoe. Each looking for a light at the end of it. Panmuir believes that his burns for peace. Meryon wants his to burn in power.' He turned now, to look at her again. 'You asked me last night if I am happy?'

'Yes.'

'I think I was evasive. But since it's no longer relevant, I'll tell you.' He moved again, went to sit on the desk. 'For a moment or two, in that restaurant, I thought that I could see a light at the end of *my* road. It was a presumptuous thought, I know, and the light was no more than a loom. But I'm a seaman and to me, in darkness, a light is something to turn on, something to give me direction.'

He was suddenly sad. 'I'd forgotten about the lorelei, hadn't I?'

'As you say, it was a presumptuous thought.'

She stood up, and Holt stood with her.

'Goodbye, Captain.'

And Holt was strangely defeated. 'Goodbye, Zoe.'

And she left, closing the door behind her.

Holt returned to his desk, sat at it and lifted a framed photograph of his two daughters. Fiona was twelve now; and Gail, eight.

But he had lost them.

As he had lost Laura.

And now Zoe.

Zoe had behaved despicably today, inexcusably, almost insanely. But Holt retained his belief in her complexity, in the thought that she was fighting some enormous and private battle. And fighting it alone. And that, he understood.

The odd thing was that – although her visit on his life had been so brief – her passing from it had left a gap. And at this time, he knew only that there were too many gaps already.

There was a knock on the door, and Napier looked in.

'Hello, James.'

'Sir.'

Holt looked at him. 'Have you seen Meryon?'

'Should thinking he's bleeding quietly, in some dark corner.' Napier shook his head, half-smiled. 'What a bitch!'

Yes, Holt thought, what a bitch.

On the face of it, that was a very fair summary.

Meryon was in fact writing a letter, and he had a picture before him, too: a photograph of his wife, Belinda.

He wrote:

'My Darling,

By the time you get this, you will have heard that I am to sail in a yacht called *Wind Song*, to oppose these nuclear tests in the Pacific. I don't know what version of my Press Conference will reach you, but the truth is that one reporter, a woman, decided to get herself a story through straightforward character-assassination.

'In as many words, she accused me of being a coward and a charlatan. And as you know, I have lived always by a policy of self-truth and self-honesty. I can admit, to my shame, that I have not been, at all times, a good husband and a good father. I can admit that, too often, my career has come before my family. But I cannot accept a charge of false behaviour, nor can I afford a question-mark against my integrity.

'And so, I am going in this boat, to prove to the world, and perhaps – I suppose – to myself, that I am worthy of my reputation and of your love. Although, in many ways, it is a desperate waste of time, it should at least underline the fact that I am willing to undergo hardship and physical testing to further the cause of peace – and that must be a point well-made for the future.'

Then he put down his pen and stared at the photograph. For suddenly, his mind racing ahead of the written words on the page, he had seen this vision for the future.

'Meryon,' they would say, 'Thomas Meryon. The man who sailed *Wind Song* into the Pacific.'

And he lifted the pen again, and squared his shoulders before returning to the letter.

And Belinda seemed to smile anew from the photograph, in love, and understanding, and pride.

CHAPTER SEVEN

TRAVAIL AND TIN HAU

In the days that followed, Holt went through an emotional wringer.

On the evening of the Press conference day, he allowed his steps (and a red Hong Kong taxi) to take him back to the market at Aberdeen. But Zoe was not there.

Twice, he went to the Excelsior and sat in the lobby-bar, sipping coke and hoping. But she did not appear.

After a certain amount of string-pulling and hard work, he got himself guest-membership of the Foreign Correspondents' Club, and visited it several times. But, apparently, Zoe did not care to eat or drink with her colleagues.

Finally, after a midnight lecture to himself and with a great deal of conscious effort, Holt elected to dismiss her from his mind – and his life – and to return to the safe, if somewhat dull, existence with which he had managed before their meeting.

But from that moment, he saw her everywhere.

In Hennessy Road, she was boarding a tram as he crossed the street only feet away.

In the Yacht Club, he saw her through a lunchtime crowd, drinking and laughing at a balcony table.

In Kowloon, while he sank his misery – and several hundreds of dollars – into a shopping trip to Nathan Road, she and Panmuir emerged from a throng on the other side of the road, and as quickly, disappeared into another one.

Once, symbolically, they passed on the decks of different Star Ferries, crossing the harbour in opposite directions.

And then, inevitably, he went through the phase in which every red-haired girl in Hong Kong was Zoe Carter – or at least, for long enough to catch his heart and dictate that first pace towards the wraith who became immediately someone else.

As the days fled away, and the date of *Wind Song*'s sailing drew relentlessly closer, a premonition of disaster began to grow out of Holt's subconsciousness, to fill his mind and sicken his heart with vague and nameless fears, and constant and increasing anxiety. Irrational as it was, the strength and persistence of the feeling were such that he was obliged to heed it, and he worried the more.

And on one hot and windless afternoon, when the beaches at Repulse Bay were filled with brown bodies and the echoes of laughter, he trecked along the sand to the huge white statue of Tin Hau, the goddess of seafarers.

Staring up into that bland, all-seeing face, he wondered what Tin Hau thought of two men and a girl, setting out in a forty-foot sloop to brave the greatest of all her oceans, and to challenge the might and right of an entire nation.

And Holt pushed fifty dollars into the narrow slit of the collection-box and lit a joss-stick to this goddess of those who ventured on the sea. He stood back, looked up again into the inscrutable face, and hoped that Tin Hau might watch over *Wind Song*, and a girl called Zoe Carter.

Someone would have to.

On the next afternoon, Christopher Panmuir was loading the last of the stores into *Wind Song* when he saw Holt coming along the jetty. Holt was dressed in a blue suit, but – as usual – was carrying the jacket over one shoulder.

Panmuir straightened from the enormous sailbag at his feet, waited until Holt reached him.

'Yes?'

'I'm Edward Holt. Captain of HMS *Hero*.'

Panmuir scowled. 'I know who you are.'

Now, he lifted the sailbag, crossed the guard-rail into *Wind Song*'s cockpit and disappeared below, into the cabin. After a moment's hesitation, Holt followed.

In the hatchway to the cabin, Holt offered: 'I came to wish you luck.'

'I can believe that,' Panmuir returned, not looking up from his work.

Holt moved into the cabin, hesitated again. 'I think you're doing the right thing. But possibly the wrong way.'

Panmuir looked at him, nodded to a bunk. 'Sit down, if you want to.'

'Thanks.' Holt sat, glanced around the tiny cabin. 'What I really wanted to do was to call on you, tell you simply that I . . . I admire your tenacity.'

'Then you're in a minority of one.' Panmuir smiled bitterly. 'In an apathetic world that doesn't care if it's – it's choked to death by pollution, or blown apart.'

Holt shook his head. 'I think that people do care. Or would care, if they stopped to think about it.'

'But they don't.'

'They may, when *Wind Song* sails.'

'Because of Meryon?'

'Because of you.'

Panmuir eyed him narrowly, got up and went to sit on the opposite bunk. 'What's your game, Captain?'

'I'm sorry?'

'You're an ex-Polaris skipper.'

'Yes.'

'And now,' Panmuir's smile was thin in disbelief, 'you want me to accept that you can have sympathy with *Wind Song*?'

'Mr Panmuir, the very fact that I did command a Polaris boat means that I've spent a great deal more time than most, thinking about the horrors of nuclear war. I can imagine nothing more terrible, nothing more futile.'

'But if you'd been ordered to, you'd have fired your missiles?'

'If I'd been ordered to.'

'So – you would have targeted hydrogen bombs on cities, on men, women, children. Wiped out whole sections of civilisation.' Panmuir looked at him, and there was contempt in the blue eyes. 'You would have *caused* the horror.'

'But don't you see?' Holt leaned to him. 'The Polaris force is a deterrent. It's in the same game as yourself – to persuade people never to use nuclear weapons. If ever we fire those missiles, we've failed. Polaris has failed. The world has failed – failed to count the cost.'

It was Panmuir's turn to hesitate. 'Are you saying . . . you *would* agree to the abolition of all nuclear weaponry?'

'I don't know.' Holt was frank. 'Emotionally, yes.' He paused. 'Realistically, I'm not sure. We've had over thirty years of relative peace. No world wars, no real invasions by the major powers. Whether they would have been so loath to go to war, if there was no possibility at all of a nuclear exchange . . . the essential point about the nuclear deterrent is that it's capable of inflicting an *unacceptable* degree of damage on any aggressor.'

'It's also capable of destroying civilisation.'

'Yes.'

Panmuir sighed. 'No-one should have to live under that kind of threat. Be asked to bring children into a world that may blow apart and kill them all in . . . in the most ghastly and agonising way. Conventional war leaves something. Flowers, trees, animals, people. But nuclear war . . .'

Holt nodded. 'That's why I admire the *Wind Song* project. Why I wish you luck.' He looked around the cabin again. 'Are you all right for stores? Medical supplies?'

Panmuir grinned. 'You'd provision a protest boat from one of Her Majesty's Ships?'

'Privately. Anything you can't get ashore.'

'Thanks. But we've got everything we need.' Panmuir smiled again. 'No room for luxuries in this little girl.'

'How many of you are going?'

'Just myself, Meryon and Zoe Carter.' Panmuir shrugged. 'They've both sailed before. And it's their decision. I was going to go single-handed.'

'I know.' Holt tried to keep it as a casual enquiry. 'And when do you sail?'

'Tomorrow morning.'

'I see.' Holt hesitated now, aware that it could all go sour on him. 'I was going to ask you . . .'

'Yes?'

'Would you consider refusing to take Miss Carter with you?'

Panmuir was surprised. 'Zoe? Why?'

'It's no trip for a woman.'

'Agreed. But Zoe is . . .'

Panmuir's voice trailed off, and the friendliness vanished. All at once, his face and his tone were bleak.

'I get it. Meryon's going on condition that Zoe goes. Stop Zoe, and Meryon may opt out.'

Holt shook his head. 'That's not the reason.'

'Like hell it's not!' Panmuir was on his feet. 'Your masters must be sweating. English politician involved in international dispute.' He glared at Holt. 'What are your orders, Captain? Stop Meryon at all costs!'

'I have no orders, Mr Panmuir.'

'Then you've got one now.' Panmuir was angry and threatening. 'Get the hell off this boat!'

Holt stood, hesitated as if about to try again, then turned and left the cabin.

Holt took a taxi down into Aberdeen village, without really knowing why.

All he knew was that Zoe was to sail on the morrow, and this was the place where he had been closest to her. A part of him said that it was a childish, schoolboyish and almost mawkish sentiment, but another part said that it was the least he could do, to appease the fear and unhappiness which continued to dwell, and to flourish, in his leaden soul.

And then he saw her.

She was waiting for him, standing in exactly the spot where they had met before. But there was no smile of greeting, no warmth in her face. She wore a short black dress and an air of defiance; and there was accusation in her voice.

'Did you know I'd be here?'

'I went down to Repulse Bay yesterday,' he answered carefully. 'Spoke to Tin Hau – the goddess of seafarers.'

'And what did she say?'

Holt risked a half-smile. 'She said that you'd be wearing that dress because you haven't room to pack it. And that while you're wearing it, you may as well go to dinner in it.'

'Nothing's changed,' she warned.

'I know.' He looked at her. 'Where shall we eat?'

'Same place.'

'Right.'

And thus, they went again to the Tai Pak. But, although Zoe mellowed slightly with the wine and the meal, Holt was as careful as before. He kept the conversation bright and non-committal until – when they were halfway through the main course – he decided that he could wait no longer.

And subconsciously, he reached for the wine-bottle and poured himself half a glass.

Zoe's eyes widened. 'Alcohol! Is it Trafalgar Night?'

'Dutch courage,' he explained.

'Oh?'

'I want to ask you something.'

Zoe was wary. 'What?'

'Don't go in *Wind Song* tomorrow.'

'I made a deal.'

'Meryon's in the part now,' Holt urged. 'He'll go whether you do or not.'

'Maybe. But unlike Meryon, I abide by my public utterances.' She smiled mirthlessly. 'I'll send you a postcard. With a mushroom cloud on it.'

Holt nodded, looked away and down to his wine glass. He played with the stem, sadness engulfing him again with the knowledge that he had lost.

Zoe watched him. 'Why did your wife leave you?'

He was forced into a half-smile. 'Who says I didn't leave her?'

'No.' Zoe shook her head. 'That would be contrary to the code of chivalry.'

'Nothing to do with chivalry – all to do with a submarine.'

'Your Polaris boat?'

'Yes.' He sipped at his wine. 'Polaris boats patrol for maybe three months at a time. Submerged. Lost. One can't even send a cable.' He paused, reflecting. 'End of a patrol, of course, there's three months on shore. But it didn't seem to compensate. My wife took it for a year and then . . . I came back from one patrol and she'd gone.'

'Did you write to her? Offer to give up submarines?'

'No.'

'Then don't ask me to give up *Wind Song*.'

Holt looked at her.

And nodded again.

In the dining-part of *Hero*'s wardroom, Meryon sat with Kiley and Wakelin, at the end of dinner. The officers were in white mess-undress; Meryon was in a black dinner-jacket; all three were finishing coffee and liqueurs.

Meryon drained his coffee-cup. 'Ah well, the last repast, eh?' He laughed, looked at his watch. 'And an early night for me, I think.'

Wakelin smiled. 'Last night for some time in a bunk that stays still, that's for sure!'

'True.' Meryon stood. So did the officers. 'In case I don't see you in the morning, before I go . . .'

He shook hands with each officer in turn. 'Goodbye and thank you for your hospitality.'

'Goodbye, sir,' Kiley said. 'And good luck.'

'Good luck, sir,' echoed Wakelin.

'Thanks.' Meryon started for the door, turned back to them. 'You know, I really believe in this fellow Panmuir. I really do think that . . .'

He broke off, reading the lack of expression in the faces of the two officers. 'Yes . . . well . . . goodnight.'

He went, opening the door to allow himself to pass out into the passage. But he had not quite closed it again when the conversation inside the mess resumed, and he heard it.

'Hell's bells!' Wakelin exclaimed. 'What a phoney!'

'Console yourself,' Kiley returned, the satisfaction patent in his voice. 'We're getting rid of him.'

And Meryon closed the door very quietly, and went away.

Holt covered yet another silence at the table by topping-up Zoe's wine-glass.

Zoe watched him critically. 'And your own.'

He smiled. 'Last glass for me.'

'And me.' She glanced at her watch. 'You'd be delighted if I missed that boat when it sails tomorrow.'

'I'd be ecstatic,' he agreed.

'Well, I won't miss it.'

There was a finality in her tone, and he looked at her sharply. All at once, he realised how near she was to going out of his life again; this time, properly: on a voyage to the Pacific, and on – to the uncharted tracts of her future. And it could be that her path would never again cross with his own journeying.

He asked: 'Has Panmuir said where he'll make for, after the protest?'

She shook her head; 'But I'll have to come back here sometime, collect the rest of my luggage.'

'And you *will* write?' he pressed. 'When you get to a port?'

'Sure.'

But Holt knew that she meant 'no', and it hurt. And it hurt even more when she added: 'Can we take separate cabs from here?'

'Yes. But . . . why?'

'I hate farewells.' She was struggling, but she forced a smile. 'Next time you're talking to your goddess Tin Hau . . . ask her for fair weather for little boats?'

'I'll do that,' he promised.

But he was still finding words, words to form another plea for her to stay, when she took him by surprise, came to her feet and kissed his cheek.

And she was gone.

And he sat on alone, among the debris of a Chinese dinner, and he felt that his life was similarly in used and discarded pieces, left-overs, unpalatable.

Suddenly, untypically, he was sorry for himself. For he saw all this as but a projection of the pattern of his past. Yet again, he would continue forward while looking backwards at what was; what might have been, what should have been; what – given time and understanding – would have been.

And he called for a brandy.

Zoe packed in a fury.

She was angry, mainly, at herself. And at her stupid decision to return to Aberdeen village, in the hope of meeting Holt.

All right, she thought, venting her annoyance on the stubborn lid of a suitcase, it had been a conscious decision, almost a calculated risk. But the result had not been as she had predicted.

And she did not know why.

She did not know why she felt guilty at her treatment of Holt.

She did not know why – despite herself – she was taken by his quixotic gallantry, impressed by his quaint and undemanding chivalry.

She did not know why it disturbed her that she had not learned more about him, obtained answers to so many unspoken questions.

She did not know why his peculiar sadness and patent loneliness had been challenges to her.

There was no element of romance in it. That, she knew. No vestige of love, lust or physical attraction. For Holt could not have been said to be the life and soul of any party: the silences had been long, if perfectly companionable, and it seemed, infuriatingly, that he spoke only when he had something to say.

She thumped the case-lid again, frustrated by her inability to analyse the feeling, antidote it and forget it. That, after all, had been the purpose of seeing him again: to identify the cause, and cure the effect.

She was long over the idea of 'some enchanted evening', and indeed, it had been far from that.

She was long over the idea that any man's company was worth the effort to keep it, and Holt was, in any event, far from being laugh-a-minute.

She had long ago taken out a subscription to the belief that ships which passed in the night should go on passing – at a rate of knots and preferably without even hailing each other.

And yet . . . and yet, with *Wind Song* and the Pacific before her, she knew only this ill-defined sorrow at leaving Hong Kong.

But she *would* leave it.

She would run away. And to hell with Holt.

And the rest of the world.

Wind Song sailed at five past nine on the following morning.

Holt, in uniform and at a vantage point on the road above the marina, watched as the little vessel filled its sails, CND burgee and red ensign fluttering bravely, and turned its back on him.

He had taken Meryon to the marina in an official car, but had been unable to bring himself to go to the boat, and he had said goodbye to Meryon in the roadway. Now, though, he could make out the three figures on *Wind Song*'s deck; and he could see the slim shape of the red-haired girl in the stern-sheets.

And he hoped that Tin Hau would do her job.

Part Two

. . . AND SUNSET

CHAPTER EIGHT

EXPRESSION OF DISPLEASURE

The weeks passed.

Hero went to sea, exercised with her main group, returned to Hong Kong. Holt received an uncomplimentary and personal signal from the Ministry of Defence, read it, tore it up. Napier chased women across the Colony, caught them, succeeded. Peek chased women across the Colony, caught some of them, failed.

Wind Song, they heard, had put into Australian New Guinea for supplies, then sailed on. But there was no card from Zoe Carter, no cable, no communication whatsoever.

And as Panmuir had predicted, the world soon forgot about *Wind Song* and got on with the business of its day-to-day-survival. Indeed, *Hero*'s main communications office logged messages from the boat for only one reason: the Captain insisted that they did.

One forenoon, some six weeks after *Wind Song* had sailed, Holt was working at his desk when Napier knocked and entered, bearing what was now a familiar length of signal.

'James?'

'Latest radio-bulletin from *Wind Song*, sir.' Napier put the signal on the desk. 'Want me to stick a copy on the notice-board?'

Initially, Holt had instructed that every bulletin from the boat was to be placed both on wardroom and ship's company notice-boards, but it became apparent, from asking questions at rounds, that no-one was reading them, and Holt was now more judicious in that he selected certain signals only.

He looked at the new message. 'Anything in it?'

'The usual anti-nuclear tirade.' Napier's tone made it clear that he had found nothing of interest in it. 'No startlingly new thoughts.'

Holt swivelled in his chair, glanced up at his First Lieutenant.

'I was thinking . . .' He hesitated. 'Sit down, James.'

Napier moved to an armchair, sat, waited.

Holt continued: 'I didn't tell you that I've had a . . . a mild expression of displeasure for my handling of the *Wind Song* business. Their Lordships were not amused.'

'What could *you* do about it?'

Holt shrugged. 'Meryon was under our wing, I allowed the Press conference in *Hero* . . . it's all caused a few red faces in Whitehall. British sloop, British skipper, British MP, British journalist, the deal set up in a British warship.'

'That,' Napier grimaced, 'was our clever Miss Carter!'

'All the same,' Holt was still strangely hesitant, 'I was wondering if we should make a signal, propose to sail *Hero*. Keep an eye on *Wind Song*.'

'What for?'

'We could sit just outside the test-area, watch proceedings. You never know – Meryon might suddenly start screaming to get taken off.'

Napier laughed. 'No way! Meryon's having a great time – addressing the world by radio.' A thin smile. 'The fact that no-one's listening doesn't seem to bother him.'

'Not yet,' Holt conceded. 'But if he got bored – or

scared – and we could haul him out . . . might improve our shares in Whitehall.'

Napier frowned. 'Are you wedded to this idea?'

'Meaning that you aren't?'

'Not much.'

'Go on.'

'Well, sir, apart from my own carnal desires, I don't like missing out on the jaunt to Japan – for the ship's company's sake. An atoll in the Pacific doesn't have quite the same facilities.'

'James,' Holt was firm, but oddly apologetic, 'I want to go after *Wind Song*.'

There was a moment's silence. Then Napier grinned: 'All right. As long as we're not ordered *into* the area. I'm too young to be sterilised by an atom bomb!'

'*Wind Song* doesn't plan to penetrate the area. Not according to Zoe Carter.'

'And you believe her?'

'I think so.'

'Strange girl,' commented Napier.

'Yes.'

'Can't blame her, I suppose.'

And Holt stiffened. And managed only the one word. 'Oh?'

'There's a story about her,' Napier went on, oblivious to the tension in his Commanding Officer.

'Yes?'

Holt got up suddenly, crossed to his coffee-maker and busied himself with a cup, keeping his back to Napier lest his expression betray his interest – and stop Napier's revelation.

'Coffee?' Holt asked, because he had to.

'No thanks,' Napier replied easily.

'Go on then.' Holt was concerned now, a dozen different possibilities about Zoe chasing themselves in his mind.

'Well,' Napier was in no such rush, 'night before *Wind Song* sailed, I think it was, Peek and I were ashore. Met up with some of the Press people, had several jars with them.'

'And?' urged Holt.

'Seems that . . . seven, maybe eight years ago, I don't know . . . Zoe Carter was teamed up with a news-photographer. Evidently, he was a pretty good guy. Looked after Zoe. Zoe was very young, adored him.'

Holt had turned, despite himself, to watch and wait. And he stood motionless, as if afraid that the slightest movement would break Napier's train of thought.

But Napier said: 'One day, outside Saigon, they were walking across a field. He was some way in front of her. Stepped on a mine.' Napier's voice dropped. 'He was blown to pieces before her eyes.'

There was another silence. Holt took the coffee back to his desk, but did not touch the drink. And when he spoke, it was almost to himself.

'Since when she's been in Northern Ireland, the Lebanon, Angola, every hot-spot in the world . . .'

Napier nodded. 'That's what they say about her. She courts death – leaves men alone.'

And yet another silence, in which Holt struggled. But, finally, he looked at Napier.

'Very well, I'll tell you because you have a right to know.' His voice became harsh, but only because he was uncomfortable. 'On the understanding that I don't normally debate my decisions, nor make them by committee.'

'Sir?' Napier was baffled.

'I'm not quite sure,' Holt confessed, 'of my motivations for wanting to go to the test-area.' He paused, then took a deep breath – and the plunge: 'I don't know whether I want to redress our errors, ease the Government's embarrassment . . . or appease my own concern for Zoe Carter.'

Napier was amazed. And unhappy.

'Sir . . . if I've spoken out of turn . . .'

'You haven't.' Holt shook his head. 'I didn't know about Saigon and the mine. But my reading of Zoe is the same as your reporter friends. And I'm beginning to understand her.'

'Then let's send the signal, get on our way.'

But still, Holt was cautious. 'We don't know what we'd be getting into.'

Napier stood up. 'All I know, sir, is that I've been through my address-book. And I'm ready to go to sea.'

Holt forced a smile. 'Must be some girls in the Colony you haven't tried.'

'All of the hunting-shooting set,' Napier assured him. 'If you hunt them, Daddy shoots you.'

Holt's laugh was one of gratitude: there were not many First Lieutenants like Napier, which was probably a good thing for the Navy. But at that moment, Holt would not have exchanged him for Lord Nelson.

The signal, in draft form, said:

FROM: HMS HERO
TO: MINISTRY OF DEFENCE (NAVY)
INFO: COMMANDER-IN-CHIEF FLEET
CAPTAIN-IN-CHARGE HONG KONG
SECRET. STAFF-IN-CONFIDENCE. WIND SONG PROJECT.
MY CONCERN WITH WIND SONG, CONSEQUENT
UPON THE VARIOUS ERRORS IN THIS SHIP WHICH LED
TO EMBARKATION OF MR THOMAS MERYON IN THE

YACHT, PROMPTS ME TO REQUEST CONSIDERATION SAILING HERO FOR TEST-AREA.

2. SUBMIT THAT IF MR MERYON SHOULD DECIDE TO WITHDRAW PARTICIPATION IN PROJECT, GOVERNMENT'S EMBARRASSMENT WOULD BE CONSIDERABLY EASED. HOWEVER, THIS CAN BE ACHIEVED ONLY IF SHIP IS STANDING BY TO TAKE HIM OUT SHOULD HE SO DECIDE.

3. HERO READY AND WILLING TO UNDERTAKE TASK, ACCEPTING PENALTY OF CANCELLED VISIT TO JAPAN.

4. CAPIC HONG KONG CONCURS IN SUBMISSION.

Captain-in-Charge Hong Kong lifted the signal and an eyebrow, looked across the desk to Holt.

'I concur, do I?'

They were in Captain-in-Charge's office, in the Naval Base, and Holt had called to win support for his plan. Fortunately, Captain-in-Charge – a tall, silver-haired man called John Warne – was a good officer and although there was a difference in their seniorities of some seven years, Holt and Warne got on well together.

Holt said: 'I want to go, John.'

'Why?'

'The signal says it all.'

'Oh, no, it doesn't.' Warne lit a cigarette. 'Do you want to go because you've had a hack in the fork from MOD, or because you feel you have a moral responsibility to watch over *Wind Song*?'

Holt hesitated. 'I have a feeling that things could go badly wrong for them. I'd like to be there.'

'In that case,' Warne smiled around the cigarette, 'I do concur. And I'll get Commander British Forces to throw in his weight, too.'

'Thanks, John.' Holt stood up. 'And the sooner we get approval, the better.'

Warne inhaled smoke thoughtfully, looked back at Holt. 'One thing, Edward.'

'Yes?'

'Don't get yourself killed for your conscience. And don't forget that you have two-hundred and sixty men in the ship – who may not see it your way.'

'I won't forget.'

Warne grinned. 'Personally, I wouldn't go within a thousand miles of that test-area.'

Wind Song was still almost two-thousand miles from the test-area.

Panmuir had proved a hard taskmaster on the other two, insisting on a rigid policy of keeping watches one-in-three, of sailing through the night, of battling on, without respite or relaxation. But strangely, and unlike Zoe, Meryon took well to the discipline and never complained.

Privately, Zoe wondered if the sun and the wind – which had burned all three of them almost black – had taken a toll on Meryon's sanity. Certainly, he appeared to have undergone some form of personality change: he was quieter, tougher, more resilient than she could have imagined.

He acted, too, as referee in the constant bickering between Zoe and Panmuir.

Most of the arguments stemmed from Panmuir's other rigid policy: that on food and water. He had rationed water from the moment they left New Guinea and he had put them now on a diet of tinned meat, dehydrated potatoes and rice – although, Zoe knew, he had canned fruit locked away.

Panmuir's ruling was that he would open the fruit in due time, when morale began to flag. But Zoe's morale had been flagging for weeks. She wanted to put into Tahiti – now about half way between their present position and the test-area – and restock with food. Panmuir, however, recalling McTaggart's experiences in *Vega*, was afraid of being arrested or delayed, on some technicality, and intended to give Tahiti a wide berth.

Yet, despite his caution, Panmuir retained absolute command in the boat and even Zoe had to admit that he was harder on himself than on his crew. Although they kept their watches and maintained a basic track on the chart, Panmuir did the real navigation and interrupted his own rest-periods to take sunsights, to check courses, even – and Zoe had to admit, too, her gratitude for it – to visit the cockpit in the night-watches and give cheer to a cold and dispirited helmsman.

In many other ways, too, he had become an inspiration to them, and had managed to instil in them a belief that they were not suffering in vain. He argued that – after the *Vega* experience, and the court actions which were still going on – no country would again take the risk of molesting another's vessel on the high seas. If they continued towards the test-area, never deviating, never losing faith, they had to win. This time, he told them, he was convinced that protest would work.

Zoe had no such conviction, but now, she did want the project to succeed – if only to justify the hours upon hours in which she had fought the motion of the boat, stifled below, burned on deck, blistered her hands on sheets and rails, and taken knocks from the boom.

In time, too, she had come to take a turn on the radio, reading from the statements prepared by Panmuir and Meryon, announcing the intentions of *Wind Song*, calling upon the world to take notice of what was happening in the Pacific. But there were moments when she wondered if anyone could hear, if there was anyone left on earth to hear, or if they three were alone on a watery planet of limitless and empty horizons, doomed to travel forever across a rolling, unending, dispiriting carpet of sea.

And in those moments, she thought of Holt. But she was no nearer to solving her puzzle. She remembered only that he had pleaded with her to stay in Hong Kong.

That had been one of his better ideas.

Holt's latest idea caused no small furore in Whitehall, and got as far as the Defence and Oversea Policy Committee, sitting at 10 Downing Street under the chairmanship of the Prime Minister.

Essentially, the problem was one of conflicting interests; and the meeting was unusually heated.

The Government, in its political self, was indeed embarrassed by the voyaging of Thomas Albert Meryon, and was more than keen to exploit any opportunity to get him away from *Wind Song*.

But the Foreign Secretary counselled caution. Putting a British frigate anywhere near that test-area, he said, was introducing an official British presence into the whole scheme of things – and that meant that the United Kingdom was acknowledging the existence of the tests, and of *Wind Song*, both of which it had been at pains to ignore.

And if the United Kingdom *did* acknowledge the tests, the Government could be expected reasonably to take some stance on the issue. But to do so would be to upset one faction or another: one could hardly condone the tests, but to condemn them would be to embarrass an important ally.

The Trade Secretary supported his Foreign Office colleague; there was no point in rocking the boat, to so speak, with a valued partner in commerce – particularly when that partner could retaliate very easily by savaging the UK over a number of trade concessions and agreements.

The Defence Secretary was nervous, too. The area was patrolled and policed by a foreign Navy. What if *Hero* became involved with them? Were there to be rules of engagement? What would happen if *Hero* was ordered away from the area – which was, technically, the high seas?

No-one mentioned the validity of *Wind Song*'s voyage.

No-one debated the morality of nuclear-testing.

No-one raised the possibility of endorsing Meryon's action.

But the Prime Minister did argue that it was the greater embarrassment to all concerned that the man was a British politician, with a seat in Government. The fact was that some might think that the Government *did* uphold Meryon's right to sail in *Wind Song.*

That, to the Prime Minister's mind, was the greater risk.

And that was why *Hero* was sailed from Hong Kong.

CHAPTER NINE

QUESTION OF RIGHTS

Holt believed always in thinking about what he wanted to say to the ship's company, before speaking on the main broadcast. He appreciated that he was addressing a large body of men, some of whom were more intelligent and better informed than others and that – while talking in simple and straightforward language – he must never talk down.

He was aware, too, that main broadcast speeches left much to be desired – there was that feeling of the Captain's remoteness, perhaps aloofness, through the disembodied voice – and that there were plenty of opportunities for the messdeck wag to run a simultaneous commentary. Indeed, he much preferred to clear lower deck and speak to the sailors face-to-face.

The problem was that – at sea – too many of them were on watch and had to rely on their fellows' translation and interpretation of what the Captain had to say. And on this occasion, he did not want that to happen.

The truth of the matter, he acknowledged to himself, was that he had a conscience. It was bad enough that he had denied the ship's company their run-ashore in Japan, and worse, that he was heading them into an area of nuclear-testing – and God knew what might happen there. But the real shame of it was that he had acted selfishly, had even falsely represented his case to the Navy and the Government, to be near Zoe Carter, and to watch over her.

The enormity of what he had done appalled him. And, because he had been reared on a diet of duty and loyalty, he felt privately that he had let down himself, his ship's company and those of his masters who entrusted him with command.

But he knew, too, that – given the same circumstances and the same girl – he would have sent the same signal and said the same prayers. Now, the only thing for which he could reasonably hope was that *Hero*'s presence in the area might eventually be justified, and a part of him was shy even of that thought, for justification could mean danger to Zoe.

Napier, on the port side of the bridge, studied his Commanding Officer, now seated in his chair and toying with the main broadcast microphone, and had a shrewd idea of what was going through Holt's mind. But there was no way in which Napier could ease that particular load. It would trouble Holt the more if he knew that Napier had read the entire game.

At length, Holt raised the microphone and spoke into it.

'D'ye hear there? Captain speaking. First of all, I want to apologise again for the cancellation of the Japanese visit. Commander-in-Chief has assured me that it will be re-scheduled, but I'm aware that the loss of it at this time has caused a lot of disappointment.

'However, we have now a very important and very sensitive task. You all know about the yacht *Wind Song*, and about her protest against the nuclear tests in the Pacific. And whatever we may think about the rights or wrongs of the situation, there can be no doubt that her crew are extremely brave and extremely dedicated people. They are also British people, and *Wind Song* is a British vessel.

'*Wind Song* does not plan to penetrate the test-area, and neither do we. Her skipper, Mr Panmuir, is in effect working a very large bluff and pinning his hopes on the embarrassment which *Wind Song* is causing.

'Now *Wind Song* is on the high seas and as such, retains the right of innocent passage. Our job will be to stand by her, and to ensure that her rights are protected. Our presence will also mean that if anything goes wrong for them, and they will be at the end of a very hard and very difficult voyage, we shall be on hand to help them.

'I won't pretend, of course, that there aren't political considerations, too. You're all aware that Mr Meryon, who lived with us for a time, is on board the yacht. But our task is to see fair play and to save life, if necessary.

'Again, I'm sorry that we've had a delay on going to Japan. But the geisha-houses will still be there next month and meantime, we'll have saved a bit more money to make the most of them.

'That is all.'

Good, Napier thought, he speaks of 'us' instead of 'you'; and he does not try to flannel them. And if there was the odd white lie thrown in, the speech was essentially honest and to the point.

Although what they could do for *Wind Song*, in reality, was another matter. Napier had seen the signals: *Hero* was to remain at least one mile outside the cordon-line, and was to approach *Wind Song* only if Meryon asked to be disembarked.

And there was no real question, if it came to it, of 'protecting her rights'.

She had none.

For all that, *Hero* went on, and at speed. She refuelled, as *Wind Song* had done, in Australian New

Guinea, then again at sea from a Royal Fleet Auxiliary tanker.

It was a long, and in many ways, a boring passage, but for Holt, it was marked by the cheerfulness of his ship's company. They had accepted, at face-value, his statement that there was a job of work to do, and perhaps lives to be saved. And that was good enough.

Not for the first time, nor the thousandth, Holt reflected that the sailor was a strange animal. Had they been sent out on an exercise – even had it been the biggest exercise for a century – the sailors would have complained incessantly, and lamented noisily their lost run-ashore in Japan. But give them a job to do – be it the Cod War or the Beira Patrol – and explain to them why it was necessary, and they would get on with it. They might not enjoy it, but they would make the most of it; and before long, messdeck humour would re-assert itself throughout the ship.

None of this, of course, helped Holt's conscience. But he busied himself with Peek in laying off a dead-reckoning track for *Wind Song*, and working out her likely position. And after nineteen days on passage, and only two hundred and fifty miles from the edge of the area, he decided to try to raise the yacht on radio.

He debated with Napier whether or not, in fact, their orders permitted them to do so.

Napier opened: 'They don't say that we can't.'

'No,' Holt was examining the signal again, 'and they don't say that we can. I suppose it depends on how one interprets "no approach is to be made to *Wind Song* unless Mr Meryon requests to be recovered from the yacht".'

He looked up at Napier. 'Verbal or physical approach?'

'If we don't tell Meryon that we're here, he won't know that he can be taken off.'

'Not by us, anyway. And there aren't many passing ferries in this part of the world.'

'Exactly, sir.' Napier grinned. 'And further to that, you've already made up your mind.'

'But at the subsequent enquiry,' Holt grinned in return, 'we can say that we did consider the matter.'

'For hours and hours.'

Holt laughed. He was excited at the prospect of making contact with the yacht.

And disappointed when, after half an hour of trying, they got no reply.

Holt, Napier and Peek returned to the chart.

Peek said: 'If he's at all worried about being intercepted, he may have swung up to the north and around this end of the area. Then he can run in from where he likes on a southerly course.'

'Yes,' Holt agreed. 'Everyone will be expecting him to be steering east-south-east.'

Napier frowned. 'But everyone's supposed to know where he is, aren't they? Isn't the idea that he bears down relentlessly on the test-area?'

Holt nodded. 'But he may be buying himself a bit of time, at this stage.' He considered. 'Paul, come port to about zero-four-zero. Whatever you think. Let's go and look for him.'

They heard it first on a BBC World Service broadcast.

Meryon had taken to listening to the news reports every day, to check for mentions of *Wind Song*. Indeed, it was an important part of their routine: they were elated when they were cited, depressed when they were ignored.

But this time, they were shattered.

The newscaster said: 'Reports are coming in from the Pacific island of Tahiti to the effect that the British protest yacht *Wind Song* has abandoned her attempt to sail to the nuclear testing-area and is now westward-bound for Australia. Mr Christopher Panmuir, the yacht's skipper, is quoted as saying that he and his crew, which includes the British MP Mr Thomas Meryon, were discouraged by the lack of interest in, and support for their activities.'

Panmuir stared at the radio-transmitter as if it had uttered blasphemy. Then he himself did.

'By Christ! We'll broadcast four times a day from now on!'

Zoe shook her head. 'The damage is done. A lot of people will tune out *Wind Song* now, on their own personal receivers. You know what they're like – they heard it on the news, so it has to be true.'

'We can come back at them,' Meryon retorted, on edge.

'Some of them,' corrected Zoe. 'Those who are sufficiently interested to listen twice. But most of them will be saying in the pubs tonight that they always knew we'd chicken. And others will believe it. And tell still more.'

Panmuir swore again, then asked more soberly: 'How the hell did it get on the BBC?'

'Easy,' Zoe told him. 'An inspired leak. Tahiti's a hell of a long way from Broadcasting House. Probably about four different stringers involved, across the world. No-one will ever trace back to where it started.'

Meryon scowled. 'We know where it started!'

'Right,' Panmuir nodded, 'and what worries me is what they'll do next. They could find us. And sink us.'

'No, Chris!' Meryon was adamant. 'They'd never

keep that a secret, and they must know it. Even a minesweeper has thirty or forty men on board. One of them, one day, would sell his story to a paper. And that would make for a very red-faced Government.'

'The French,' Panmuir reminded him grimly, 'rammed *Vega*. And then claimed that it was *Vega* who threw herself under the bows of *La Paimpolaise*.'

'But if we're supposed to be heading for Australia,' Zoe argued, 'no-one can claim that we suddenly popped up at the test-area, or anywhere near it, and got rammed.'

'No!' Panmuir was impatient. 'They know that story won't last. Not officially. That's just to get on our nerves, teach us that we're up against the big boys, persuade us to throw in the towel. But if we go on, and if we keep up our broadcasts, someone may decide to clobber us. Run us down at night. If we're all drowned, who's to say that I didn't turn across their bows?'

'Chris,' cautioned Meryon, 'you're putting an awful lot of store on what McTaggart *said* about *Vega*. The French officers had a different version.'

'There were photographs. Of the beating-up.'

'Photographs,' Meryon was gentle, 'don't necessarily prove a thing.'

Panmuir stared at him. 'McTaggart spent *twelve days* – under guard – in Papeete military hospital; because, the French said, he slipped on the deck of *Vega*.' His face clouded in despair. 'Who's going to slip on the deck of *this* boat?'

Zoe looked at him, reading the hopelessness in the tired, drained face. 'Chris, you're not thinking of giving up?'

'No, But I *am* thinking . . . I wish I'd refused to take you two along.'

'Oh, come on!' Meryon was brisk, confident. 'This is exactly what they intended with that news release! To get us down. Frighten us with their size and their expertise.'

'Precisely!' Zoe was more bloody-minded than brisk. 'And to hell with them. There's no story in turning back!'

'You know,' Panmuir half-smiled to her, 'I still couldn't say what's really on that mind of yours.'

'Canned pears for supper,' she answered firmly.

Panmuir stared at her. Then laughed. 'All right. Break out the canned pears!'

'A number of you,' Holt said into the main broadcast microphone, standing on the darkened bridge, 'will have heard a report on the World Service that *Wind Song* has given up and is now on her way to Australia.

'But ten minutes ago, we picked up a bulletin from the yacht which makes clear that she is still headed for the test-area and still intent on making her protest.

'Our task remains, therefore, and we are now moving north-east in an attempt to make contact with *Wind Song*. I'll let you know as soon as we're successful.

'That is all.'

As Holt replaced the microphone, Napier crossed the bridge to him, said: 'His transmitter must be more powerful than his receiver.'

Holt nodded. 'I should think it is. He needs the transmitter to get his bulletins out, but I don't imagine he expected to get many calls.'

'Did we get a DF bearing on the transmission?'

Holt nodded again. 'Zero-four-seven from us.' He looked at Napier. 'Of course, anyone else who was listening would have got a bearing, too.'

'And anyone else with two sets of DF equipment in different places . . .'

'Would have got a fix.' Holt grimaced, looked at his watch. 'Well, we should sight her tomorrow forenoon.'

He glanced to Peek, at the chart-table at the back of the bridge. 'I'll be in my cabin, Paul.'

'Aye aye, sir.'

'Goodnight, James.'

'Goodnight, sir.'

Holt left the bridge, went down to his cabin and poured himself a coffee. He was tired, but excited again at the thought that he might see Zoe, albeit through binoculars, on the morrow.

He smiled wryly as he took the coffee to an armchair, and sat. Hell of a thing to have chased a girl almost nine thousand miles.

And for all he knew – after so long, literally, in the same boat – she could have fallen for Panmuir.

He frowned. Panmuir. He had a feeling that Panmuir was in a corner now. Or would be, very shortly. At the moment, as they had agreed, Panmuir was buying time: circling the area and keeping out of everyone's way while continuing his broadcasts and his appeals. There was not much time left, however: the first bomb was due to detonate in about thirty-six hours, and before then, Panmuir had to make a decision.

It had been a brave try, to sail to the very edge of the area while pleading for political action and world indignation, but Holt had never really believed that it would work. Nor, he fancied, had Panmuir.

He accepted, in Zoe's words, that 'Panmuir's not going to get himself fried for his cause. And sure as hell, Thomas Meryon isn't'. That was not the point. The fact was that Panmuir's next logical step was to escalate the bluff and cross the cordon-line. And once he had done that, he was into a very dangerous game. He could be arrested, or molested, or both, and Holt could not cross the line to find out. Or – if he got the arithmetic wrong – he could be caught in the blast and killed.

Holt wondered what was in Panmuir's mind.

And Zoe's.

And all of a sudden, a thought struck him with such force that he moved abruptly in the chair, the coffee slopping unheeded on to the white sleeve of his mess jacket.

It was a possibility.

It had worried him incessantly that Zoe had been quite so vicious to Meryon at the Press conference. There had been in her an unnecessary and unnatural desperation. But how important had it been to Zoe that Meryon went in *Wind Song*?

In the event, the challenge for herself to go had come from Meryon; but had it not, would she later have used Meryon's presence in the yacht as a lever on Panmuir to take her, too?

He could not believe that Zoe had thought it all out, consciously. And he was sure that her shock at Meryon's counter-thrust had been genuine. But on a subconscious level, had there always been that fascination with *Wind Song*'s journey?

When other journalists had written their two lines of copy, and moved elsewhere, Zoe had gone back again and again to the little boat. But why?

Could it be, because nuclear bombs were the most devastating weapon in death's great armoury? Had the dark shape of death, hanging over the atoll, been a magnet to her, a waiting lover to the complex and guilt-ridden machinations of her solitary, uncommunicative mind?

He did not know. He did not understand, for he had never lost a loved one in such traumatic and soul-scarring circumstances.

But he did know now that his primary feeling for the girl was one of protectiveness: a desire to turn her from her lonely, bitter road; to drag her out of the shadows and point her towards the sun.

That was why he was here.

CHAPTER TEN

MAYDAY

Panmuir had handed over the watch to Meryon at four in the morning, but had remained in the cockpit until dawn began to lift out of the eastern horizon. Then, he had gone below – but, it seemed to him, he had no soooner touched his head to a pillow than he was awake again; and was hurling himself from the bunk in response to Meryon's scream.

'Chris! Chris! There's a ship bearing down on us!'

Zoe was already out of her bunk, but Panmuir reached the cockpit first, pushing Meryon out of the way and heaving himself up and out of the cabin.

And his heart stood still.

It was a minesweeper. But it looked to be as big as an aircraft-carrier as it came at them, racing in at right-angles and pointing directly at their starboard beam, its white bow-wave curling against the grey bow – like a row of teeth in a shark's mouth.

Panmuir hurled himself at the tiller, knowing even as he did so that he was not going to make it.

But at the last second, the minesweeper altered to port and went under *Wind Song*'s stern. Only just. The yacht rocked violently to the ship's wake and the cockpit was suddenly awash in water.

Zoe screamed.

Meryon cursed under his breath.

Panmuir watched as the grey shape of the sweeper, one hundred and fifty feet long and four hundred tons, went hard to starboard and passed up the yacht's port side. He could read her number – M681 – and see bare-chested figures on the sweepdeck.

He swallowed, tasting the fear, licked his dry lips and told Meryon: 'Check our position, Tom. Make sure we're still outside the area.' He grimaced. 'I *know* we are, but check it all the same.'

And as Meryon dropped into the cabin, Zoe warned tensely: 'They're coming in again!'

They were. This time, the sweeper turned from right ahead and came directly at the yacht, bow to bow, on a reciprocal course. Panmuir went rigid, his hand frozen to the helm. For he had no idea what to do – and it did not help that his mind was numb with terror.

The most elementary rule of the road at sea demanded that a vessel under power give way to one under sail. The next most elementary was that two vessels in this position should both turn to starboard, to open. But was this it? Was the sweeper waiting for *Wind Song* to turn starboard, that she might turn port and cause an unfortunate but effective collision?

Zoe snapped him from his immobility. 'For Christ's sake, Chris, do something!'

Panmuir threw over the helm, to turn the yacht to starboard, at the same time scrabbling in panic for the main sheets. But the sweeper had already altered to her starboard. Only five degrees or less. But enough to take her narrowly down *Wind Song*'s port side, again sending her wash inboard and lashing Zoe and Panmuir with face-stinging spray.

A last desperate glance at the sweeper, now turning in a wide arc to bring herself ahead of the yacht again, and Panmuir dived down into the cabin.

Meryon looked up from the chart. 'We've got at be at least fifty miles from the cordon-line.'

'Right.' Panmuir snapped a switch on the radio-transmitter. 'This'll do a hell of a lot of good, but sooner or later, that fellow's going to make a mistake – deliberate or otherwise – and we'll be at the bottom of the sea.'

He lifted the handset, spoke into it.

'Mayday, mayday, mayday! This is British yacht *Wind Song, Wind Song*. Under attack on the high seas by a foreign warship. Mayday, mayday, mayday!'

And the impossible happened.

After only a few seconds' pause, the receiver crackled and a calm, very-British voice said: '*Wind Song*, this is HMS *Hero*. Roger your last. Have been trying to call you. Hold you and bandit vessel on radar. Closing you best speed from the south-west.'

They stared at each other.

'*Hero*,' breathed Panmuir.

Meryon smiled. 'The Government must have sent her from Hong Kong!'

'Someone did,' Zoe agreed obliquely. 'And we'd better concentrate on staying afloat until she gets here!'

They scrambled in a crush for the hatchway. For a moment, incredibly, they had forgotten the minesweeper.

On the bridge of *Hero*, Peek was conning the ship and Holt and Napier stood together, talking in low tones, at the starboard side.

Napier asked: 'Are you going to tell MOD about the mayday?'

'Not yet.'

'In case they say no?'

'I don't see that they could.' Holt was staring out ahead. 'We're answering a distress message, from a British vessel on her lawful occasion on the high seas.'

'But that vessel,' Napier reminded him, 'is *Wind Song.* And we've been told not to approach her.' He looked at Holt. 'And not to get involved with ships patrolling the area.'

Holt half-smiled. 'Are you suggesting that we ignore a mayday, James?'

'No!' Napier was horrified at the thought. 'I'm a rebel, remember? It's good enough for me that the MOD wants us to play it quietly – I'm going to get out my big drum.'

Holt smiled anew. 'Boasting again!'

But, in fact, he was worried. He was all too aware that he should send a flash signal to the Ministry of Defence, reporting the situation and seeking instructions. But to do so would be to surrender the initiative which he retained as a free agent; and there was a risk – however small – that he could be told to stand off while Foreign or Defence Ministers chatted to each other in their circuitous ways.

Then Peek said: 'Ships visual ahead.'

Holt took his glasses, trained them above the bow and felt his heart lurch to the sight of a white sail. But there was a darker shape ominously close to it. He looked to the Chief Yeoman.

'Chief, challenge that warship ahead. By light.'

'Aye aye, sir.' The Chief Yeoman left the bridge in a hurry, went to the bridge wing and turned on the big signal-lamp. He sighted on the distant warship and sent: 'What ship?'

The minesweeper replied: 'Minesweeper *Isis.* M681.'

Holt ordered a further signal: 'This is Her Britannic Majesty's Ship *Hero*. It has been reported to me that you have been harassing the British yacht *Wind Song*.'

A long pause from *Isis*. Then: '*Wind Song* requested assistance. I have been attempting to take her in tow.'

Holt looked to Peek. 'Are we plugged to *Wind Song* on voice?'

'Affirmative, sir. Channel six.'

Holt moved to the starboard side of the bridge, took a handset from the signalman, turned up the loudspeaker.

'*Wind Song*, *Hero*. Captain Holt.'

'*Wind Song*, Panmuir.'

'Good morning, Mr Panmuir. The *Isis* claims that you asked for assistance and she was merely trying to put a line on you.'

'I know, Captain.' Panmuir sounded almost amused. 'I can read morse, too.'

Holt half-smiled. 'Do you require help of any kind?'

'No,' Panmuir answered strongly. 'All I need is a bit of sea-room to get on my way.'

Conscience pricked Holt again. He had another job to do, too. 'Is Mr Meryon all right?'

'Mr Meryon is fine.'

'And Miss Carter?'

'Fine, too.'

'Roger, standby.' Holt put down the hand-set, looked again to the Chief Yeoman. 'Make to *Isis*. "Thank you for your offer of help. I shall look after *Wind Song* now. Please do not let us detain you further".'

There was an even longer pause this time. Then *Isis* flashed: 'You must encourage *Wind Song* to withdraw. If she strays into the test-area, we cannot be responsible for what may happen to her.'

Holt responded: '*Wind Song* is outside the test-area. She has the freedom of the seas.'

And *Isis* returned, more quickly: 'For the moment.'

Then water churned white at the minesweeper's stern as she got underway, swung to port and moved off to the south-east.

And Peek kicked *Hero* closer to *Wind Song* and Holt could see Zoe Carter on deck. She was wearing a white T-shirt and blue shorts and her long red hair was being teased by the wind.

Holt smiled, fondly and to himself, and moved to the bridge wing. He angled the fitted loudhailer at the yacht, then took up its microphone.

'Mr Panmuir.'

Panmuir, in the stern-sheets of the yacht, lifted a hand.

'I'll speak to you this way because *Isis* may be monitoring our radio conversations.'

Panmuir raised a hand again.

'What way do you intend to go now?'

Panmuir pointed east-north-east.

'Roger. *Isis* is opening to the south-east at about ten knots. I suggest,' Holt felt vaguely treacherous, but he was not sure to whom, 'that you lower your radar-reflector now and get on your way, tracking north first for about five miles. After that, there should be no danger that *Isis* can pick you up or know where you've gone.'

Panmuir gave a thumbs-up and even as Holt watched, Zoe and Meryon started to unship the radar-reflector. Without it, a small yacht such as *Wind Song* would not paint on radar until the intercepting ship had almost fallen over her. Certainly, she would be lost to the *Isis* in a matter of minutes.

Holt spoke into the microphone again. 'I shall remain

here until you are well clear and I'll keep a radar watch on *Isis* to ensure that she doesn't turn back.'

He hesitated. He had been told not to approach the yacht, and certainly he should not offer any form of succour or comfort. That *could* put the Government into a difficult position, and leave embarrassing questions to be answered.

But they were a long way from Whitehall. 'Can I send anything across to you in my sea-boat? Cigarettes, beer, milk, anything?'

Panmuir shook his head, waved his arms in a negative gesture.

Holt smiled thinly. He had expected no other answer: a man had to have a certain amount of pride and independence to come this far.

And he watched as *Wind Song* filled her sails with the south-westerly wind, turned north and drew away. And he used binoculars to keep them in sight until he could no longer distinguish the white of Zoe's shirt.

Zoe and Meryon were almost ebullient after the *Isis* incident, the knowledge of *Hero*'s presence lifting their spirits and giving them fresh heart.

But Panmuir was withdrawn. He had taken himself down into the cabin and he sat there alone, deep in thought and desperately depressed.

For him, the *Isis* incident had confirmed only one thing: he was afraid. Of physical force, of violence, of being crippled, of being killed. His whole campaign was for life without fear, without violence, without the terror of nuclear holocaust. Because, he understood now – and indeed, had always suspected – he was unable to live with the threat of pain or destruction.

That was why, he accepted bitterly, he had not committed himself and his boat to the whole course. He had devised a plan whereby he would go to the edge of the area, and the edge only. For the beatings and the harassment and the collisions were sure only inside the cordon-line. Outside it, he had thought, in his smugness and stupidity, they might have left him alone.

So what now? Give up? Go home? Forget his principles and the people who had raised four thousand pounds to send him as their champion?

Damn it, he was afraid!

There was just one chance left. One small, remote and face-saving chance.

He went back into the cockpit, sat opposite Zoe and Meryon, looked at them for a long moment.

'I'm going to make another broadcast,' he said at length. 'To the effect that if no announcement is made within the next twelve hours, to say that the tests have been cancelled, *Wind Song* will cross the cordon-line.'

'Good!' Meryon was still confident.

'The thing is,' Panmuir hesitated, fighting his own fear, 'if there is no announcement, I'll have to go in.' He was struggling. 'I'm not going to be stupid about it. I'll sail along the edge of the area, just inside the line. They must have some kind of safety-margin, they don't just draw lines on a map. But technically, *Wind Song will* be inside the area. And they'll have to let off their bomb with a foreign vessel inside their designated danger zone.'

Meryon nodded. 'Seems sensible.'

'It isn't!' Panmuir was almost savage. 'A strong tide, a shift of wind, anything – and we could be in trouble.' He looked at them again. 'What I'm saying is . . . *Hero*'s here now. I could ask her to take you both off.'

Meryon actually laughed. 'You're not serious! We've

come nine thousand miles with you, and you're asking us to abandon you for the final twenty?' He laughed again. 'It's . . . it's like flying from New York to London and asking for a parachute over Heathrow, because you're afraid of the landing!'

As before, Zoe was amazed. Meryon had changed so much on the voyage, had found an inner strength, a calm, a sense of humour which seldom failed him.

But she was amazed, too, at herself, and at her own reaction. Of a sudden, she was confused and uncertain.

She wanted to follow Meryon's example, to come back at Panmuir with a smile on her lips and a light-hearted rejoinder. But she had seen Holt again this very day, and Holt, inexplicably still, seemed to stand for so many other things. So many other chances. And the great adventure was all at once a gigantic gauntlet, to be run only – now – in the knowledge that there was very definitely another way to go.

But Panmuir was looking at her, she knew. And she took a breath, met his eyes and grinned.

'It's all a plot,' she said, 'to keep that canned fruit for yourself!'

Holt had plotted, too, and had reported the *Isis* incident in the terms that *Hero* had received a mayday, gone to the assistance of a yacht. The yacht had proved to be *Wind Song*, and already had *Isis* standing by her. *Hero* had ascertained that the yacht was safe, after all; and had taken the opportunity to confirm that Mr Meryon did not want to be recovered. *Hero* had then thanked *Isis* for her assistance, and all three vessels had parted company.

He was pleased with his signal, which was perfectly truthful in so far as it went, and his humour put a smile around his coffee-cup – until Napier knocked and came in, carrying another signal.

Napier said: '*Wind Song*'s threatening to penetrate the area. Unless the tests are cancelled. She'll go in at midnight and she'll stay until the bomb is detonated.'

Holt's smile vanished with his humour. This was what he had expected. And had hoped against.

He took the signal from Napier, nodded. 'Leave it with me, James.'

'Sir.'

But Holt did not bother to look at the signal. When Napier had gone, he leaned back in his chair, drank more coffee and faced the thought which had been uppermost all day in his mind.

Hero might have to go into the area, too.

And transit nuclear fall-out.

CHAPTER ELEVEN

HEROES AND DREAMERS

In theory, it was hazardous, but not impossible.

A British warship is so constructed that a large area within the ship, known as the citadel and usually comprising all main internal compartments, can be sealed off from the outside world by means of gas- and water-tight doors, flaps and hatches. All fans are switched to recirculation, which means that no air is drawn from the outside atmosphere (which would be contaminated), and the ship's company breathes only the relatively fresh air taken into the ship before closing-down, and recirculated for as long as is necessary.

Before entering a fall-out zone, a system known as 'pre-wetting' is put into operation, activating a variety of hoses, pipes and nozzles on the upper-decks, causing a constant flow of water across all weather areas – and hopefully, washing off most of the contamination into the sea.

The ship's company – apart from men on watch – go to 'shelter stations', which puts them as deep into the ship as is possible, in order that each steel bulkhead or deckhead between them and the radiation will increase the 'shield factor' and lessen the effects of any harmful rays.

For further protection, everyone wears an anti-gas respirator, anti-flash hood and gloves, and long-sleeved shirt and long trousers (or overalls).

If anyone has to leave the citadel (for example, monitoring and decontamination teams), he is allowed to re-enter only by passing through a cleansing station, in which he is undressed by specially-trained men (his clothing will be ditched or properly treated before re-issue) and made to scrub himself thoroughly under a shower.

Having transitted the fall-out, therefore, the ship's company should be still alive and relatively well; and – as soon as the monitoring parties have checked the upper-deck and declared it free, life should go back to normal.

In theory, Holt reflected again. But in reality, it could be a nightmare of gamma radiation, beta skin-burns, sear and blindness, sickness and death.

And again, he questioned his motivations. Was he considering taking *Hero* into fall-out to save life? Or to save Zoe Carter?

He recalled Captain-in-Charge's caution: 'Don't forget that you have two-hundred and sixty men in the ship.'

But he had not forgotten. Nor had he forgotten that it was, traditionally, the Navy's duty to be 'a security to those who pass upon the sea on their lawful occasion'. How lawful was this occasion, he was not sure. But there were three people in *Wind Song*, three Britons. And he was the Captain of a British warship, almost on the spot. He had to be prepared, at least, to be their security.

If he was so permitted.

He drew a signal form to him, wrote:

FROM: HMS HERO
TO: MINISTRY OF DEFENCE (NAVY)
INFO: COMMANDER-IN-CHIEF FLEET
SECRET. WIND SONG HAS DECLARED INTENTION OF

ENTERING TEST-AREA AT MIDNIGHT LOCAL TIME AND REMAINING UNTIL NUCLEAR DEVICE IS DETONATED. THIS DETONATION SCHEDULED FOR NOON LOCAL TIME TOMORROW. INTEND THEREFORE TO BE CLOSED DOWN TO NBCD STATE ONE CONDITION ZULU ALPHA BY MIDDAY TOMORROW AND TO REMAIN AT EDGE OF AREA. IF WIND SONG THEN CALLS FOR AID FOR WHATEVER REASON, PROPOSE TO ENTER AREA TO SAVE LIFE AND EFFECT RESCUE IF POSSIBLE.

He read the signal through, changed the 'propose' to a second 'intend' and had the message despatched.

Then, he called a briefing meeting in the day-cabin.

It was attended by Napier, Peek, Kiley, Wakelin and Greg Scarf, the Marine Engineer Officer. Napier, of course, knew what to expect; but – Holt was aware – the others were going to be horrified.

He adopted, therefore, a brisk and business-like style and began: 'I wanted to brief you before I tell the ship's company. *Wind Song* is not very far away, as you know, and has now announced that if the tests are not cancelled by midnight tonight, she'll cross the cordon-line, enter the area and stay put until the bomb goes off.'

He looked around them. 'My feeling is that whatever *Wind Song* may do or say, those tests will go ahead on schedule.'

'Sir,' Kiley was anxious, 'if the bomb does go off . . .'

'*Wind Song* may still be safe,' Holt finished. 'My guess is that Panmuir will have done his sums. And he won't get so far in that he can't race out again, ahead of the fall-out.'

'Won't he be in an upwind sector?' Scarf asked.

Peek shook his head. 'The test-area is a long key-hole shape, running east-north-east from the atoll. That's because the prevailing wind is from west-south-west. Panmuir is somewhere on the northern edge of the keyhole, probably about a third of the way down by now.'

'So presumably,' Napier said, 'he'll dodge out again by going north when the bomb drops?'

Peek nodded now. 'If he goes any other way, he's dead.'

Wakelin was appalled. 'But if his sails are burned off, he's becalmed, he suffers blast damage—'

'Exactly,' Holt agreed, cutting into Wakelin's catalogue of disasters, aware that they could all be uncomfortably accurate. 'If for any reason, he gets caught, he may need to be rescued.'

He had thrown it in, almost casually. And there was a moment of silence before it hit the officers.

Then Peek spoke for them, his jaw dropping: 'By *us*?'

'It's possible,' Holt said, affecting calm.

'But, sir,' Peek was still horrified, 'how would we get to *Wind Song*? Around the perimeter, or cutting the corner?'

'Cutting the corner. We'd have to get there as fast as we could.'

Peek's jaw fell again. 'But . . . that could take us through some fairly heavy fall-out!'

Holt nodded. 'We've practised transitting nuclear fall-out often enough. But I agree that the real thing's a different matter.'

He looked to the two technical officers. 'Greg and Bill, you'll have to be on the ball. It's not good enough that the citadel is airtight but for one dodgy door down aft. The interior of this ship has to be sealed off totally. Recirculating air *must* recirculate. Citadel pressure *must* be retained.'

To Napier. 'James, we must be able to close down quickly and efficiently, with not one flap or hatch forgotten. Every man must know his shelter station, carry a personal dosimeter. And the pre-wetting must work.' He glanced at Scarf. 'The firemain pressure must be able to wash off the upper deck, not just dribble over it.'

To Wakelin. 'Monty, your cleansing-stations must be able to *cleanse.* That doesn't mean passing people through showers and getting them wet. It means a really good scrub, an efficient system for dumping contaminated clothing, a proper check before people get back into the citadel.'

To Peek. 'Paul, we'll run the ship from the Operations Room, of course. But I want a sharp radar look-out, the full teams closed up, yourself on the con.'

He leaned back. 'Now, let's hope we don't go in. But let's be prepared. I'll make a broadcast now to the ship's company and we'll have a full exercise in an hour. And another at nine in the morning. Any questions?'

Wakelin voiced everyone's thought: 'All it needs is one mistake.'

'One mistake,' Holt concurred, 'one slip in the drill, one breach of the citadel – and we'd recirculate nuclear fall-out instead of air.'

He stood up, and the officers came to their feet, too, as he looked around them again. 'Impress that on the ship's company. All of you. Tell them that if we obey the rules, we'll make it. But if we break them . . . remind them that Panmuir's right about one thing: nuclear radiation isn't selective. We blow this one and we're all dead.'

It was almost midnight. The yacht was hove-to, and Zoe, Panmuir and Meryon were in the cabin. Arguing.

Or more precisely, Zoe was arguing with the other two.

As time had marched on towards their deadline, and there was no response whatsoever to their ultimatum, both Panmuir and Meryon had expressed disappointment and disgust.

And Zoe, in an odd mood and still privately torn by conflicting emotions, had let rip at them.

'I can't understand,' she exclaimed, 'why you think you had a chance with that idea!'

'We might have got a postponement,' Panmuir said.

'Oh, rubbish! And going into the area's not going to make any difference, either. They'll still let off their bomb.'

Meryon frowned. 'I'm not sure. Dreadful thing for any country to do. Detonate a nuclear explosion when they *know* there are people in the way.'

'Look,' Zoe was even angrier now, 'we *are* talking about a country, a nation. They're not going to be held to ransom, change their Defence policy, because of three insignificant people in one insignificant boat! They can't afford to. No country could. If they allowed that kind of precedent to be set, it would open doors for cranks from ... Portsmouth to Penang.'

Meryon sighed. 'We've got to try.'

'We're going to try,' vowed Panmuir.

Zoe shook her head. 'All right. But you're both out of your minds if you think it'll matter a tuppenny damn to anyone. So let's not have a wake tomorrow, when there's a big bang. There's nothing we can do about it.'

'Zoe,' Panmuir was tired, 'shut up. Please.'

He looked at his watch, came to his feet. 'Time's up. We're going in.' And to Meryon: 'Tom, prepare a statement and get it off, will you? Keep it short, in case they're direction-finding.'

'Right.'

Meryon moved to the radio-desk and Panmuir went past Zoe, and up into the cockpit.

Zoe stayed where she was, rubbed her eyes, shook her head again. She was being a bitch, she knew, but it angered her that – even now – the two men would not accept the futility of what they were trying to do. If – as she had told them – there had been some possible chance that their gesture could have affected the issue, she would have seen the point in their risking the crossing of the cordon-line. But that bomb would go off, even if there were a dozen *Wind Songs* tied up to the atoll itself.

Besides, she admitted, she was afraid. And fed up. All her life – all her life since Vietnam, anyway – she had been running. Away from something, towards something; she could not say. But suddenly she wanted to stop, to admire the view, to have doors opened for her, chairs held for her.

Damn Holt! It could never work. He would want someone in buttons, bows and laces, in long dresses and floppy hats, in some sweet little cottage near a Naval Base.

Her lips turned down in sourness. She must be going out of her mind.

With fear, she supposed.

It was all right for Chris Panmuir. He had no nerves at all.

She glanced up through the open hatchway to the cockpit. He would be up there, racing *Wind Song* for the cordon-line.

Yes, she thought again, it would be all right for him.

But it was not all right. His hand trembled on the helm, and there was sickness rising in his throat. He had tried initially to tell himself that McTaggart had taken *Vega* into the test-area. And then he had remembered what had happened to McTaggart. Twelve days in hospital.

And the sweat broke out again.

Zoe was right, of course. It was a waste of time, because it would change nothing. The bomb would go off. And he would go home. As McTaggart had gone home. And Ingram. And Davidson. And all the rest.

And he would promise to try again next year.

Or the year after that.

But those years would be filled with the memory of that minesweeper, bearing down on them at speed; and he would taste again the terror and the defeat.

And he would make excuses, and delay yet another year.

Some men were heroes, and some were dreamers.

Too bad that he had to choose a job in which he should have been both.

Napier knocked on the day-cabin door at half an hour after midnight. He was dressed in a pair of white overalls and there was a dirt-smear on his cheek. He looked exhausted.

Holt got up from his chair and went to take a bottle of brandy from a cupboard. He said: 'Sit down, James. You look wrecked.'

'I don't know why it is,' Napier said, dropping into an armchair, 'that sailors have to paint *everything*. Pre-wetting nozzles, half the rubber sealing-strips on the screen doors, hinges on machinery-space ventilation flaps.'

Holt was pouring the brandy. 'Will it all be ready? In time?'

'Oh, it'll be ready. Nothing gets a man working harder in the middle watch than if you tell him he'll be dead if he doesn't.' Napier took the brandy. 'Thanks. The good thing is – very few of them have dripped.'

'About working? Or the possibility of fall-out?'

'Fall-out.'

Holt smiled thinly. 'I can't believe that.'

'It's true. It's also true, of course,' Napier admitted with a grin, 'that the NBCD Manual's never been so popular. Even the Canteen Manager's had a copy.'

Holt laughed. 'And the sailors aren't twitched?'

'They're twitched. They're not daft. But they aren't moaning. Not about the job, anyway.'

'Meaning?'

'Well,' Napier hesitated, 'there are one or two of them who seem to believe that nuclear-protesters should be like climbers. If they get themselves stuck on a mountain, they've no right to ask others to risk lives in getting them down again.'

'Any of the officers thinking like that?'

'Couple were. They've now been given the order of the Napier boot.'

Holt hesitated now. 'What about you, James? Truthfully.'

'Me?' Napier sipped at the brandy, grinned again. 'I reckon it could have great advantages in the future.'

'Oh?'

'When you throw her into bed,' Napier explained, 'and she says "no, no, I might get pregnant", you say "don't worry, darling, I was in *Hero* in the Pacific when the whole ship's company got sterilised".'

Holt shook his head, smiled to his First Lieutenant.

'Doesn't *anything* frighten you, James?'

Napier considered. 'Growing old. The taxman. Admirals' wives.' A pause. 'Nuclear explosions.'

'It does frighten you?'

'Scares the hell out of me.'

Holt nodded. 'Me, too.'

CHAPTER TWELVE

COUNTDOWN

Ironically, it was a beautiful morning.

With a hot sun on his face and a cool breeze at his back, Panmuir sailed *Wind Song* across an empty ocean; but miles behind, there was an invisible line on the surface of the sea. And by traversing it, he had exchanged peace for peril.

Once, in the night, he had seen the lights of a ship – probably the dreaded *Isis* – far to the west. But the lights had continued to draw away, and he had breathed again.

Now, well inside the area, it was simply a question of waiting for time to pass – yet again. And of praying for the ultimate miracle, for an announcement that the tests had been postponed.

For even a postponement would have given him the excuse to pull out and claim a victory in part. But he knew that no announcement would come, and he settled himself to steering the yacht and waiting for the others to finish breakfast.

He himself had been unable to eat.

Peek checked the log, looked up again and spoke into the conning-microphone.

'Stop both engines.'

He turned to Holt, in his bridge-chair. 'Ship stopped in planned position, sir. One mile outside the area.'

'Very good.' Holt put down his coffee cup. 'Are you maintaining your DR plot for *Wind Song*?'

Peek nodded. 'Yes, sir.' Then added with a grimace: 'But I haven't really got a clue where she is. I laid off a track from where we met her yesterday. North for five miles, then east-north-east until midnight last night, then south-south-east into the area. But Gods knows where she went after that. Or where she is now. Or if she was hove-to for part of yesterday.'

Holt smiled encouragingly. 'All right, Paul.'

Peek was unhappy. 'Sir, forgive my asking, but I don't see why we can't head east-north-east as well. Then stop at a mile from the edge of the area, at the point where I think she went in. Then, if she does come up and call for help, we may not have to cut the corners to get at her.'

'Perfectly valid,' Holt conceded. 'But if we go north-east, it could indicate what part of the area he's in, to the *Isis* and the others. By staying down here, more or less where we've always been, we keep them guessing.'

'I see, sir.' It was on the tip of Peek's tongue to query if it was *Hero*'s function to confuse the patrol-boats; but he thought better of it: he had been savaged in the Wardroom last night, by Napier of all people, for asking a similar question.

And then Napier appeared, from below, and crossed to Holt. 'I've started closing down the ship, sir. So that when we go to zulu alpha, about twenty to twelve, there won't be much to do.'

'Right.' Holt reached for a signal clip-board. 'Seen this? From MOD?'

'No, sir.'

Holt handed across the signal. It referred to Holt's earlier message about a possible rescue, then said:

APPROVED. HOWEVER YOU ARE TO REMAIN CLEARLY OUTSIDE THE AREA, AT A DISTANCE OF AT LEAST ONE

MILE, UNTIL THE EXPLOSION HAS OCCURRED. THEREAFTER YOU MAY ENTER, BUT ONLY TO SAVE LIFE AND DEPENDENT YOUR PERSONAL ASSESSMENT OF CONDITIONS PREVAILING AT THAT TIME.

Napier snorted. 'In other words, "you suggested it. Don't blame us if you get it wrong".'

'It's fair,' Holt defended. 'They could have ordered us to stay out whatever happens.'

'Yes,' Napier grinned fiercely. 'And that would have given us a problem.'

They exchanged glances and Holt smiled, wondering if Napier believed his Captain to be a rebel, too.

Then Holt started, lost his smile and stared at the wind gauge by his left knee.

Napier's eyes followed Holt's. 'What is it, sir?'

'The wind. It's freshening.'

Peek looked, too, at the wind gauge. 'And backing, sir. It's now from about two-three-five.'

Napier was anxious. 'That could wreck Panmuir's arithmetic.'

'And dump a whole load of fall-out on him,' Holt agreed, 'much quicker than he expects.'

Peek said: 'He must have noticed. He's a seaman, in a sailing yacht.'

'He may have other things on his mind today,' Holt returned drily, and looked to Napier. 'James, go down and call him. You probably won't raise him, because we know his receiver's weak. And even if you do, he probably won't acknowledge in case he gives away his position.'

'Right, sir.'

Napier left, and Holt leaned back in his chair, patently worried.

He hoped the message would get through.

It did not.

But, in fact, Panmuir had noted the change in the wind, and could hope only now that the same wind which would carry the fall-out faster, would also drive him quicker to safety.

He was in the cockpit of *Wind Song*, with Zoe. He looked to her, asked: 'You know the explosion's due at midday local time?'

'Yes.'

'Ten minutes before, we'll all go into the cabin, get dressed properly. Cover arms, legs, heads; tuck the bottoms of our jeans into our socks.'

Zoe stared at him. 'Why? The jeans and socks, I mean.'

'Because if we get sear off the explosion and your ankles aren't covered, you'll be walking around without feet for the rest of your life.'

Zoe stilled a shudder, swallowed hard. And when she could trust herself to speak, she queried: 'Are we in *real* danger, Chris?'

'Ask me at one minute past twelve.'

'You mean,' she was still staring, 'you don't know?'

Meryon was coming out of the cabin, to join them. Panmuir glanced at him, then told Zoe: 'We'll get down in the cabin, we'll dress, close the hatch, stuff up all the vents with rags and things. When the explosion's happened, you and Tom will stay in the cabin. I'll come out quickly, close the door again, turn her north and set the course.'

'And,' she could hear the waver in her own voice, 'if we're on fire?'

'We'll put it out,' Meryon supplied calmly.

And Panmuir nodded. For now, he did not trust himself to speak, either: if they were on fire, God help them.

By eleven-forty, the bridge personnel in *Hero* (and indeed, everyone else in the ship) had undergone a radical change of uniform. Gone were the bare torsos, the white short-sleeved shirts, the shorts, the sandals. In their place, both officers and ratings wore a long-sleeved blue shirt, buttoned to the cuffs and neck, long action working dress trousers, with bottoms tucked into socks, shoes, anti-flash hood and gloves, anti-gas respirator in carrying-satchel, lifejacket clipped around the waist, personal dosimeter clipped to shirt-pocket (to register each man's personal dosage of radiation).

And the atmosphere on the bridge was tense as Holt nodded to Napier.

Napier crossed to the main broadcast, pressed the main broadcast alarm and allowed it to run for several seconds, then switched it off and spoke into the microphone.

'Assume NBCD state one condition zulu alpha. I say again, state one condition zulu alpha. Dress of the day is full number eights or overalls, with anti-flash gear and lifejackets. AGRs and personal dosimeters are to be carried. The ship's routine is now being run from the Operations Room.'

And it was, for by the time he had replaced the microphone and turned for the stairs, the bridge was empty. He stood for a moment, conscious of the eeriness, then hurried below.

But it was eerie, too, in the Operations Room. Always dark, to enable the operators to read the radar pictures, it was now unusually quiet. There were no contacts to report, no submarines to chase, no aircraft to engage.

Yet there was the full first team closed up here, waiting, watching, wondering, lost in private thoughts, unwilling to shatter the silence with a single, deafening word.

Holt was suddenly tired, suddenly suffering from the burden of responsibility which he felt both for *Hero* and for *Wind Song*. And very soon, there might be a clash of interests there: the need to go in to save *Wind Song*, and the knowledge that to do so would be to hazard *Hero*.

He tried to close his mind to what might happen to that little boat, and to the girl within her frail hull; to the possibility that there would be no radio message from *Wind Song*, ever again. It did not help that they had no real idea where the yacht was, how close she might be to the blast, how heavily she would be contaminated before – and if – they had a chance to get to her.

For one awful and vivid moment, Holt had a mental image of what could be; of three sets of the cinders of humanity, scorched and charred and scarred, floating unrecognisable on a watery bed of radiation.

And he gripped the arms of his chair, and fought away the image and the nausea.

And prayed.

In the cabin of *Wind Song*, Zoe and Meryon had plugged the vents and then dressed themselves to accord with Panmuir's instructions.

Panmuir himself came down from the cockpit, closed the hatch and door, lifted a sweater off a bunk. All while Meryon found the courage to tell him.

'Chris . . . there's just been a radio warning. The explosion is confirmed for five minutes' time.'

Panmuir nodded. 'Then we've failed.'

Zoe looked at him, and there was no way that she

could ever have said 'I told you so'. For there were the tears of frustration in his eyes, and the desperation of defeat in his face.

But he spoke steadily: 'I've rehoisted the radar reflector, maybe prove to someone that we're really here.' His voice had started to crack with the last word. He cleared his throat, said: 'We'll all get down on the deck in here now. Face aft. Cover your eyes and your face in your hands.'

He watched as the other two got down, and he reached a hand and touched each, briefly and encouragingly, on the shoulder. Then he lowered himself to his knees, by the hatchway to the cockpit and he closed his eyes.

But the tears squeezed through.

He got down properly on the deck, buried his face in his hands, pleaded with himself not to be sick.

Meryon thought of Belinda, his wife. And his three children.

Zoe thought of Holt.

And Holt thought of Zoe, as he watched the second-hand of the Operations Room clock sweep through eleven-fifty-nine and start its countdown to horror.

He looked to Peek. 'Pilot, how long will we take to get to *Wind Song*? At twenty-five knots?'

'I'd say . . . about two hours, sir.' Peek fiddled with dividers on his dead-reckoning chart of *Wind Song*'s position, amended: 'Two hours, ten minutes if she's where we think.'

Holt grimaced. Decided.

'Get us underway, Paul. Take the ship up to the edge of the area. We'll save that mile at least.'

He glanced back at the clock. Twenty-five seconds to

go. He was not really breaking orders: by the time the screws started to turn, and got the ship moving forward, the bomb – suspended in its balloon, high above the atoll – would have been detonated.

And if he *was* breaking orders, he no longer cared.

In the yacht, Panmuir had been unable to keep his eyes closed, for the fear had built in the silence, and from not knowing how long there was to go.

He had synchronised his watch with a radio time-signal that morning, and now – for no other reason than the need to hear the sound of his own voice – he was counting down for the others.

'Five . . . four . . . three . . . two . . . one . . . zero.'

He plunged his face into his hands.

There was a second of silence; a second which stretched to an age.

And then the bomb went off.

CHAPTER THIRTEEN

GOLDEN DAY

In the Operations Room, there was a moment of silence and stunned horror.

Holt was the first to recover.

'Estimated bearing of *Wind Song*?'

Peek snapped to reality. 'One-two-eight, sir.'

Holt glanced up at the gyro-repeat. 'Come left to one-two-eight. Revolutions for twenty-five knots.' He hesitated. Then: 'Correction, twenty-eight knots.'

As Peek gave the orders over the conning-microphone, Napier did a mental check on the terms of the MOD signal. It had said that *Hero* could enter the area only to save life, but it had also said that Holt could make a personal assessment. Clearly, Holt had assessed that there was life to be saved.

And Holt, reading Napier's thoughts, told him quietly: 'If they're in real trouble, the call for help may never come. And we may have to close the distance before they can hear us.'

Napier nodded. His stomach was tight now, and he could see the strain in every other face in the Ops Room. Except Holt's. And he was determined that, equally, he would give nothing away.

He lifted the main broadcast microphone, and raised an eyebrow in enquiry to Holt.

'Please,' Holt said simply.

Napier spoke into the microphone: 'Hands to shelter stations, standfast men on watch.'

And into the red NBCD telephone: 'Switch on pre-wetting.'

They were on their way.

Panmuir lifted himself off the cabin-deck, and discovered that the other two were staring at him – as if seeking confirmation that they were still alive.

He discovered, too that he was shaking uncontrollably, and he clasped his hands one in the other, and clenched his teeth.

Meryon said gently: 'At least, we tried.'

'Yes,' Panmuir agreed, in a strange, stricken voice, 'but who'll remember next week?'

He shuddered, caught himself, told them: 'Stay here.'

He opened the hatchway, went through, closed it again and levered himself into the cockpit. His first emotion was one of relief: the sails were still there; the boat was not on fire.

He looked first to the east, and it was still a beautiful day.

And to the west.

The great cloud hung in the sky, billowing, spreading, reaching out for him. Even now, perhaps, the first rays were bombarding him, the first layer of deadly dust settling on his skin, and in his lungs.

And he had a vision of a razed land. Of withered grass, and bare hills, and polluted rivers, and stilled cities, and death everywhere. Cattle in the fields, canaries in their cages, babies in their cots, children in their play-grounds, women in their kitchens, men in their innocence.

He hauled in the sheets, to turn the boat, and there were tears in his eyes. It was such a terrible, hideous, revolting evil, unstoppable in its stalking of all things living, indiscriminate in its taking of life, torturing in its lingering, vomiting, racking but inevitable death.

Unstoppable.

But he had tried. God, he had tried.

And to the east, it was a beautiful day.

A golden day.

But to the west . . .

And suddenly, through the tears, through the fears, through the terrible tragedy of it all, he knew that there was but one answer.

And that, in truth, was no answer at all.

And it terrified him.

But greater than the terror was the tiredness. The emptiness. The knowledge that he would never have the courage to come back and try again.

He had fired his last sling-shot, and Goliath was still standing. McTaggart, Panmuir . . . how long a line would it be?

He had to believe that there *were* others; waiting, slings ready. And that one day, one of them – somehow – would floor the giant. That all that they needed was a call to arms, a rallying-point, an example – as McTaggart had been an example to him.

But he would do more than McTaggart. A little more, at least. And sound a trumpet in the distant Pacific.

He was too tired to do anything else.

And he got up again, and went down once more into the cabin. Zoe and Meryon looked at him questioningly, alarmed. But he smiled absently and went to the radio, lifted the hand-set.

'*Hero, Hero*, this is *Wind Song, Wind Song*. Over.'

And Holt's voice. '*Wind Song*, this is *Hero*. Captain Holt. Over.'

'*Hero, Wind Song*. Panmuir. Read you weak but clear.

Request rescue operation as soon as possible. Over.'

'Roger, *Wind Song*.' Holt's voice, Zoe thought, was calm and reassuring. 'Can you give me your approximate position? Over.'

'Approximately five-zero miles south-east of our meeting-point yesterday. My radar-reflector is up. Over.'

'That's fine, and puts you more or less where we thought you would be. I'm already closing you from the north-west at best speed. Request you steer north-west to meet me. Over.'

Panmuir's knuckles whitened on the hand-set. 'Sorry, Holt. I'm not giving ground. I'm stopping in my present position, and when you've got the others off, I'm going on.'

Zoe and Meryon were on their feet. Meryon cried: 'No, Chris!'

Into the hand-set, Panmuir rapped: 'Over and out!' Then he looked to Meryon. 'I've got to, Tom. The only way *Wind Song* is going to be remembered is if someone dies – if their nuclear explosion actually kills someone.'

Meryon stared at him, tears in his own eyes.

'Chris . . . for God's sake, don't react emotionally.'

'I'm not.' Panmuir shook his head. 'I'm scared. Very, very scared. Any minute now, I'm going to weep. But I do know what I'm doing.'

Zoe was dry-eyed, coldly angry but deeply concerned. She said savagely: 'Don't be a fool! Those bastards aren't worth it!'

But Meryon spoke very quietly.

'Chris,' he was pleading, 'have you thought about it? About . . . about death by radiation?'

'Yes.' Panmuir looked at Zoe, and his voice had gone. 'And that's where you come in, girl. You wanted a story and now you've got it. Make it graphic. Make it horrible. Make it so sickening that they throw up at their breakfast tables!' The tears were on his cheeks. 'Make them think, Zoe. Just make them think!'

And Meryon came and put an arm around Panmuir's shaking shoulders. It was an odd gesture from the once-aloof and remote politician; but it was simply, Zoe knew, a heart-felt attempt on Meryon's part to transfer his strength to Panmuir.

Meryon began again: 'Chris . . .'

'No!' Panmuir shook himself free, and stood.

'Ask Zoe,' he said. 'Defeat is commonplace. But death is news.'

Holt, Napier and Peek were gathered at the Ops Room-chart-table when Kiley, in white overalls and wearing his gas-mask, entered the compartment. He looked around, saw that all personnel were wearing masks – except Holt, Napier and Peek. And he removed his own, to register his disapproval and to speak clearly.

'Sudden and rapid increase in radiation level, sir.'

Holt frowned: 'Danger level? Outside?'

'Yes, sir.'

'Right.' Holt nodded to himself, in confirmation of an earlier thought. 'I'll coxswain the gemini myself. I'll need one volunteer to go with me, handle the passengers and—'

'You've got one,' Napier told him.

Holt hesitated. 'One of us should stay.'

Napier shrugged. 'Paul knows the ship better than I do.'

Holt hesitated again. It was quite wrong for both Captain and First Lieutenant to leave the ship at the same time, at sea. Particularly in nuclear fall-out – when both might go down ill as a result, and leave the ship in the hands of a junior officer for the return passage across the Pacific. But he needed someone with him who would stay calm, keep the gemini dinghy alongside *Wind Song* for as long as was necessary, settle Zoe and Meryon and help steer them into the cleansing-station.

'All right, James. Gemini lowerers?'

'Volunteers standing by, sir.' Napier was business-like. 'And I've already fixed decontamination-suits for you and me.'

Holt half-smiled. And lost the smile as he thought of Panmuir.

Panmuir was in the cockpit when *Hero*, still pre-wetting and streaming water from her scuppers, grew out of the horizon and came up at twenty-eight knots, to stop at a hundred yards on the yacht's starboard beam.

Almost immediately, figures appeared on the flight deck; figures that looked grotesque and unwieldy in their protective clothing, hoods and gas-masks. And within minutes, they had swung the little rubber gemini outboard on its davit, and lowered it into the water.

As Panmuir watched, a jumping-ladder was dropped to sea-level and then two men, anonymous in the shape-less suits, clambered down the ladder and got into the dinghy. One of the men carried four satchels and took control, starting the outboard engine.

Panmuir waited until the dinghy was on its way, then went back to the cabin.

Thus, the yacht was deserted when Holt put the dinghy alongside and climbed inboard, still carrying the satchels, while Napier held the gemini against *Wind Song*.

Holt went through the cockpit and down into the

cabin. He pushed up his own respirator, held out three satchels to the trio opposite him.

He spoke rapidly, urgently. 'Respirators, for what they're worth now.' And to Zoe and Meryon: 'Put them on, and get in the gemini. Quickly as you can!'

Meryon smiled, almost apologetically.

'I'm staying in *Wind Song*, Captain. With Mr Panmuir.'

Stunned, Holt looked from Meryon, to Panmuir, to Zoe.

Zoe said desperately: 'Stop them! They're both idiots!'

Holt grimaced, asked Meryon: 'You're sure? You know I can't come back?'

Meryon answered obliquely. 'You should have your mask on, Captain. Don't risk your life to argue with us.'

'For Christ's sake,' Zoe yelled at Holt, 'tell them they're mad!'

Holt slammed a respirator into her hands, countered roughly: 'Put it on! Get in the boat!'

Instinctively, Zoe bridled.

Holt snapped: 'Now! Hurry up!'

Zoe looked quickly to Panmuir and Meryon, swallowed hard, managed: 'Goodbye!'

She went out fast, struggling with the respirator.

Holt turned back to the other two. 'You know that you'll probably be intercepted?'

Panmuir nodded: 'They'll try. But I'll unship the radar reflector again as soon as you've gone.' He sounded exhausted. 'They won't get to us until it's too late.'

Holt lifted the fourth satchel, passed it to Panmuir.

'Medical satchel. There are some ampoules of morphine . . . in case. And I put in a Bible.'

'Thank you,' Panmuir acknowledged simply. For there was nothing more to say.

And Holt looked into the pale and haunted face, and he held out his gloved hand.

Panmuir took it in silence.

Holt turned, looked again to Meryon.

'Why?' he asked softly.

'I don't know.' The smile flickered anew on Meryon's lips. 'But some time ago, someone called me a phoney. And out here . . . I got to realising that he was right.'

'Your career? Your work?'

Meryon shrugged. 'Who was it who said . . . "ambition should be made of sterner stuff"?'

He clasped Holt's hand.

'Goodbye, Captain.'

Holt's look embraced them both.

'Goodbye, gentlemen.'

Panmuir returned to the cockpit for *Hero*'s departure, and he watched as the ship got underway and turned north, for safety.

The symbolism of the manoeuvre sent a lump into his throat, and he fought it as he fought the sudden wash of pain and loneliness. And he knew that, but for the quiet and brave man below, he would be now on the radio, pleading with *Hero* to return, his nerve and his dignity in tatters.

That was why Meryon had stayed. That Christopher Panmuir, self-appointed martyr and coward extraordinary, might die as he had contracted to die; and not end this last of all journeys in scorn, discredit and disgrace, screaming into the radio and shaming himself and his beliefs before the world.

For the final broadcasts had to be controlled, and

reasoned, and clear. And without Meryon, without the man's support and succour, he could not achieve them.

It was odd, Panmuir thought, watching the disappearing frigate, that – by becoming friends and sharing loyalties – he and Meryon had each assured the demise of the other. But perhaps, even in this, no man could stand entirely alone.

He coughed, and wiped his mouth with the back of what he knew was already a dying hand: the great cloud was overhead now; spilling its lethal load on to the yacht as surely as the tears spilled once more on to his cheeks; sliding a dark and final lid across the sky to close off the sunlight of life; casting not a shadow but a stain, not on the sea but on the whole planet.

This was what he had to remind himself. That he was dying, not so much that others might live, but more that there might be a heritage for future generations; that, indeed, there might be a future.

There was a poem that he wanted to recall, and he could not. There were things that he wanted to see, and never would again. There were dreams that he had cherished, and were gone forever. And there were memories, that remained.

Of a girl with dark hair, whom he had loved unrequited. The park at Richmond, which he had walked in snow. A night in Paris, and lights in the rain. A concerto by Mozart, and a song by Neil Diamond. A film called *Love Story*, and a book called *The Once And Future King*. A boat called *Wind Song*, and a damned great minesweeper making him sick with fear.

So he would do it. Shoulder to shoulder with Meryon, he would bear the suffering and the agonies and the eternal night to come, that others might see in that night a small and far-off star – but not so small, and not so far-off, that it could not guide them. And perhaps, one day, through its inspiration, its example, guide a misguided world and turn its people from a course of self-annihilation.

That was the hope and the prayer; and hope and prayer were all that remained.

Now, the sky was darker. The air was colder.

But somewhere, it was a beautiful day.

A golden day.

CHAPTER FOURTEEN

FACE OF THE DEEP

Well briefed by Wakelin, and conscious that this was the real thing, the cleansing-team had wasted no time on concessions to Zoe, and embarrassment for her womanhood. They had stripped her of her clothing, watch and jewellery, and had monitored her carefully after she had showered and scrubbed.

And when, with Holt, she passed naked into the citadel, Wakelin himself was waiting for them. He handed them their respirators (now decontaminated, by another team), pushed up his own and gave Holt a pair of overalls, socks and shoes, and Zoe a dressing-gown.

Holt, expecting more substantial clothing for Zoe, looked queryingly at Wakelin.

The Supply Officer explained: 'I want Miss Carter to go to the officers' bathroom, sir, and scrub again.'

'Beta skin-burns?' Holt asked.

'Maybe.' Wakelin, here, was very much in charge. 'We took you through the boundary cleansing-station quickly, because the damned thing's topped up with radiation itself. But that means that the cleansing may have been inadequate – for anyone who wasn't in protective clothing.'

'I had my respirator off,' admitted Holt. 'In the yacht.'

Wakelin looked disapproving. 'In that case, sir, same drill for you.'

'So you're accepting some decontamination,' Holt frowned, 'within the citadel?'

'For the time being.'

'All right, Monty.'

Zoe, depressed and understanding almost nothing of the exchange between the officers, allowed herself to be led for'ard by Holt, waiting as he unclipped and re-clipped door after watertight door, and to the officers' bathroom. They showered in silence, were monitored again for radiation, allowed to dress again in fresh clothing – this time, white overalls for both.

Holt broke the silence then, saying: 'Let's go down to the Ops Room.'

And it was then, in the empty cabin flat, that Zoe wheeled on him, eyes blazing.

'You could have stopped them!'

'There was no time for arguments or debate, Zoe.' Holt was firm. 'Another five or ten minutes and we'd have been in the irreparable-damage stakes. Even now, with a less-efficient cleansing-officer, we could have been in trouble. And for all I know, still are.'

Zoe was insistent. 'You could have stopped them!'

Holt sighed, confessed. 'I had no intention of stopping them.'

'Why not, for Christ's sake?'

'Zoe . . . I told you once before. We're each on our own road. Those two men know where they're going.' He looked at her. 'More important, they know why.'

'Don't moralise with me! I tricked Meryon on to *Wind Song*!'

'But he stayed of his own free will.'

She shook her head. 'I have to live with it. Thanks to you, I have to live with the knowledge that—'

'Zoe!' He rapped out the word, startling her. 'Stop collecting other people's deaths. And start living your own life!'

She stared at him, and he was disturbed: she was still dry-eyed, as she had been on the yacht. Not a hint of a tear. That shell was still around her. After all this . . .

He said gently: 'Panmuir and Meryon are giving their lives for their beliefs. But you're wasting yours – because you're afraid to believe in anything.'

'You've let them die!'

'No, Zoe,' he denied. 'I let them choose.'

And he went through the hatch, down the ladder and into the Operations Room. And after a moment, she followed.

Napier was already in the Ops Room, having been faster through the cleansing-process, but Peek still had the con.

Holt looked at him. 'Course, Pilot?'

'Three-five-five, sir. Speed twenty-four.'

'And *Wind Song*?'

'Two-zero-zero. Speed four.'

So. Panmuir had honoured the promise, and gone deeper into the area.

Holt glanced again to Peek, asked: 'Are we still in radio-contact?'

'Should be, sir.'

Holt moved to the radio hand-set and Napier, gentle fingers on the girl's elbow, steered Zoe and himself to join Holt.

Holt had the hand-set at his lips, was about to depress the transmit-key – and hesitated.

He had said goodbye. What else was there to say?

That they would be remembered. But would they?

That their sacrifice would not be in vain. But might it not?

That part of him was guilty that he had not gone

with them. Was that not too easy to say from here – when the greater part of him was very glad that he was going the other way?

That the name of *Wind Song* would dwell in the annals of courage. For a whole week?

And if he did call them, make contact, how could he phrase a final farewell? It was not as final as theirs.

And he lowered the hand-set and placed it, almost reverently, on the table before him.

Then he looked up at Napier, met his eyes.

Napier nodded in sympathy, responded in a hoarse whisper: 'What does one say . . . at the end of the world?'

And they three – Holt, Napier and Zoe – stood in silence. And then the voice crashed in on them from the loudspeaker. Meryon's voice, still recognisable on radio. Rich, loud, echoing.

A voice that filled the dim, tense Operations Room and brought every other man to his feet, to straighten in unconscious salute and to listen in sorrowful awe.

For clearly, Meryon could find a message, at the end of the world.

He said: 'In the beginning, God created the heaven and the earth. And the earth was without form and void.

'And darkness was upon the face of the deep . . .'

EPILOGUE

Napier read Holt's draft signal. It said:

AT FOURTEEN-FIFTEEN LOCAL TIME TODAY, HMS HERO RECOVERED MISS ZOE CARTER FROM THE YACHT WIND SONG, DEEP INSIDE THE NUCLEAR TEST-AREA, AND SHORTLY THEREAFTER TOOK LEAVE OF TWO VERY BRAVE AND VERY FINE MEN.

2. MR CHRISTOPHER PANMUIR AND MR THOMAS MERYON HAVE ELECTED TO REMAIN IN THE AREA UNTIL THEIR DEATHS BY RADIATION-POISONING, AS A PROTEST AGAINST THE TESTS AND AN APPEAL FOR THE ABOLITION OF NUCLEAR WEAPONRY.

3. I HAD THE PRIVILEGE, I BELIEVE, OF BEING THE LAST MAN TO SEE THEM ALIVE. I WISH TO RECORD, THEREFORE, THAT THEY WENT TO THEIR DEATHS WITH DIGNITY, CONVICTION AND AN UNSHAKEN BELIEF IN THE VALIDITY OF THEIR CAUSE.

4. HOWEVER ONE VIEWS THEIR CAUSE, AND WHETHER OR NOT ONE ACCEPTS ITS VALIDITY, ONE IS MOVED TO BELIEVE THAT WHILE MEN LIKE THESE WILL SACRIFICE THEIR LIVES FOR THE ABOLITION OF STRATEGIC ARMS, THAT CAUSE MUST FINALLY TRIUMPH OVER NUCLEAR WEAPONRY'S USERS AND PERPETUATORS, WHO MUST BE PREPARED TO KILL BUT MAY NOT BE PREPARED SIMILARLY TO DIE.

5. MY OFFICERS AND SHIP'S COMPANY JOIN ME IN OFFERING DEEPEST SYMPATHY TO THE RELATIVES OF PANMUIR AND MERYON, AND WE WISH TO STATE THAT OUR TOO-BRIEF ACQUAINTANCE WITH BOTH IS A SOURCE OF PRIDE AND HUMILITY TO US ALL.

Napier frowned.

'That,' he predicted, 'is going to get up a lot of noses, back at the ranch. Especially coming from an ex-Polaris Commanding Officer. If the Press ever got hold of it . . .'

'That's an idea,' Holt said.

And in defiance, he added:

6. I WOULD BE GRATEFUL IF THE FULL TEXT OF THIS SIGNAL IS RELEASED THROUGH THE DIRECTOR OF PUBLIC RELATIONS (NAVY) TO ALL OUTLETS IN PRESS, RADIO AND TELEVISION.

'Send it off.'

And Napier took the signal, and went.

And Holt returned to his concern for Zoe.

But that concern eased slightly on the following day.

At dusk, with the ship well clear of all things nuclear, and with the upper-deck free again, Holt made a broadcast to the effect that he would hold, in five minutes' time, a brief memorial service for Panmuir and Meryon. He stressed that he was not clearing lower deck, and that he would expect to see only those who wished to attend.

But, save for the men on watch, the entire ship's company came to the flight deck, packing it all the way back to the after guard-rails.

Holt was obliged to climb to the sea-cat deck, where the ship's company could see and hear him, and he stood flanked there by Zoe and Napier.

And he conducted the service; a short, simple affair that had no pretentions to be other than it was: the homage of fighting men to two warriors fallen in a great if one-sided battle.

For all that, it was very moving, and many heads remained bowed for longer than was necessary, and many feet were shuffled on the flight deck.

But Zoe stayed dry-eyed.

Then, in conclusion, with the sun dipping red into the western sea and with darkness throwing a fittingly-sombre cloak around the ship and its mourning company, Holt quoted a passage from Binyon's *For the Fallen.*

'They shall not grow old,
as we that are left grow old:
age shall not weary them,
nor the years condemn.
At the going down of the sun
and in the morning
we will remember them.'

And he looked to Zoe.

And at last, she had broken. The shell had not yet shattered, perhaps, but it had cracked. And she wept in racked sobs.

And Holt lifted his eyes to the sky, and thanked God.

She would be all right.

FUTURA CASH SALES,
110 WARNER ROAD,
LONDON S.E.5

Please send me the following titles

Quantity	SBN	Title	Amount
______			______
______			______
______			______
______			______
______			______
			______
		TOTAL	======

Please enclose a cheque or postal order made out to FUTURA PUBLICATIONS LIMITED for the amount due, including 10p per book to allow for postage and packing. Orders will take about three weeks to reach you and we cannot accept responsibility for orders containing cash.

PLEASE PRINT CLEARLY

NAME...

ADDRESS..

....